CULEBRA CUT

CARIBBEAN SEA
(ATLANTIC OCEAN)

CANAL

CULEBRA CUT
(NOW GAILLARD CUT)

ZONE

Culebra

N

PANAMA
CANAL

PACIFIC OCEAN

CULEBRA CUT

BY JUDITH HEAD

CAROLRHODA BOOKS, INC.

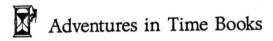 Adventures in Time Books

Text copyright © 1995 by Judith Head
Cover illustration copyright © 1995 by Mary Quinlivan
Diagrams and map copyright © 1995 by Carolrhoda Books, Inc.

Carolrhoda Books, Inc. c/o The Lerner Group
241 First Avenue North, Minneapolis, MN 55401

LIBRARY OF CONGRESS CATALOGING-IN-PUBLICATION DATA
Head, Judith.
  Culebra Cut / by Judith Head.
    p. cm. — (Adventures in time)
  Summary: When his father takes a job as a doctor with the Panama Canal project in 1911, William, who is fascinated with the canal, gets to learn about it firsthand, while he also learns about life from a Jamaican girl who has become his best friend.
  ISBN 0–87614–878–X
    1. Panama Canal (Panama)—History—Juvenile fiction. [1. Panama Canal (Panama)—History—Fiction. 2. Blacks—Panama—Fiction.] I. Title.
II. Series.
PZ7.H34225Cu   1995
[Fic]—dc20
                                                    94–32023
                                                        CIP
                                                         AC

Manufactured in the United States of America
1 2 3 4 5 6 – BP – 00 99 98 97 96 95

For my daughter, Austin,
and husband, Michael

CHAPTER

O N E

William Thomas pushed out the screen and climbed onto the windowsill. Dawn skirted the horizon and coated the sky with faint light. William grinned as he thought how close he was to his dream. Soon he would stand at the edge of Culebra Cut and watch as thousands of workers and machines carved the Panama Canal out of the mountains.

An explosion from the Cut shook the heavy, damp air. William took a breath and jumped down onto the wet grass. The screen slapped against the window frame. He froze, listening for sounds of his parents stirring, but heard nothing.

The world outside was alive with noise. A monkey's

howl cracked the air. A bird warbled a melody, and another answered. A soft hum droned near William's ear. He wiped the side of his face with his hand and was relieved to find only a thin layer of sweat.

Around his feet the moist air thickened into fog. Careful to keep his eyes on the ground, he headed for the boardwalk behind the house, then quietly followed it among the other dwellings. Where the buildings and boardwalk ended, he stepped off into the thick, wet grass.

Another explosion thundered in the Cut. He pictured the dirt and rock being tossed up and tried to run toward it. Matted grass grabbed at his shoes. Wet air filled his lungs. Sweat dripped from his face and tickled his back between his shoulder blades. He hardly noticed.

Where a foot-wide crack split the ground, the grass gave way to mud. William jumped the gap, and slippery, blue-black clay oozed into his shoes. He pulled his feet free and stepped back onto the grass. Ahead of him the ground disappeared under a dense mist.

"The Cut!" he said excitedly. "It's got to be."

For William being at the site of the largest construction project in history was a miracle. More than a year before, his neighbor, Mr. Fergueson, had served a stint as an engineer on the canal railroad. He had begun sending William issues of the *Canal Record*, the weekly newspaper of the Isthmian Canal Commission, or ICC, and William was hooked. He pored over the facts and figures in each issue: the amount of concrete in the canal's six gigantic locks, the number of cubic yards of earth in the breakwater at Colón, the water level of the lake behind Gatun Dam. He pictured the plows scraping fill from trains of flatcars, cheered as Culebra Cut deepened, and grieved at each report of a slide sending dirt and rock tumbling into the Cut. To William an issue of the *Record* was more exciting than an adventure story by Jack London.

During the summer of 1910, when Mr. Fergueson had returned home to Maine, William's father was exhausted and ill. A hard winter traveling on skis or snowshoes to tend patients had been followed by a cold, wet spring spent digging his buggy out of the mud. Deep creases lined Dr. Thomas's face, and a cough rumbled in his chest.

"Get away to a warmer place. Panama's the answer," Mr. Fergueson had suggested. "Every one of those villages along the canal has got either a dispensary or a small hospital. Plus there's a huge hospital complex in Ancon. The ICC is always short of doctors. There may be some mud to wade through, but you'll never see a snowflake. And most of the patients will come to *your* door."

William was jubilant. "We've just got to go. It'll be as important as watching the Egyptian pyramids being built. You'd want me to see that, wouldn't you?"

His father hesitated. "Who will care for my patients?"

"Get someone up from Boston to take them on," Mr. Fergueson replied.

At first Mrs. Thomas had protested. "Panama may be warmer, but it's got diseases like yellow fever and malaria. And with all the construction, living near that canal must be dangerous too."

"You don't have to go down into the chasm, and I'll give you a gold piece for every mosquito you find within a mile of a canal town" was Mr. Fergueson's retort. "Colonel Gorgas and his crew have wiped out Yellow Jack. Besides, it's the adventure of a lifetime."

William did not know whether his pleading or his father's lingering cough was more persuasive. But after a July day of cold, pelting rain, his father had come around. "I don't think I can take much more of this bad weather. And who could pass up a chance to see the canal—and to be paid for it."

William's mother agreed. "Working there has got to be easier than being the only doctor in half a county."

The decision made, Dr. Thomas took a position at the small hospital at Culebra. William was overjoyed, because the town was the site of ICC headquarters and the hub of operations for the Cut. But there was a catch—he would have to obey certain rules.

Now, in July 1911, on his first full day in Panama,

William stood at the edge of Culebra Cut, the most challenging stretch of the whole canal. He was sure that no place on earth teemed with excitement and purpose like the spot where the Big Ditch was being carved through the mountains. But he had already broken his parent's most important rule—that he never go near the Cut alone.

CHAPTER

T W O

William stared into the twisting mist. Soon the advancing sunlight and the breeze from the sea would lift it right out of the Cut.

For hundreds of years people had dreamed of digging a canal through the narrow isthmus of Panama. Eliminating the long voyage around South America would make travel between the Atlantic and Pacific Oceans much faster. In 1881 a French company attempted to fulfill that dream. They made plans to dig a canal at sea level. But almost as soon as work in Culebra Cut had started, wide sections of the bank across from the village of Culebra began sliding toward the bottom. The slides, as well as problems with money and disease, forced the French to give up the project in 1899.

Four years later the United States signed a lease for a ten-mile-wide Canal Zone across the isthmus. The ICC scrapped the idea of a sea-level canal in favor of a lock model, which would allow digging in Culebra Cut to stop at forty feet above sea level. Even so, the slides were getting worse.

William looked behind him. The houses were only shadows, but a shape like a giant serpent loomed close in the haze. Flatcars! William rushed to the line of train cars standing ready for loads of dirt, then hurried toward the end of the line.

A huge Bucyrus steam shovel, its massive jaws at rest, sat wrapped in fog. Beautiful, he thought, as beautiful as anything nature could produce. And it was powerful too. "Five cubic yards a bite. Ninety-five tons—so big that it takes ten men to run it," he announced to the mist. William knew why the steam shovel was there: to take off the top of the mountain so that it could not slide into the Cut.

A piercing whistle blasted, making William jump. Another joined it. He rushed back to the rim. Beneath the swirling fog, boilers popped, engines bellowed, shovels clanged. Steam merged with mist. The work day had begun.

William knew that his father would already be at the

hospital for his first day of work. His mother would probably look into his room to check on him. He hoped the lumps in his bed were convincing.

Gradually the haze lifted to reveal the great gash. Along the opposite side of the Cut, on the sheared cliff that years before had lain deep within the mountain, layers of orange, pink, purple, and red earth blazed in the sun. Here and there, strands of deep green foliage crept down from the hilltops like fingers intent on taking back the land.

Not far below, a steam shovel lay on its side. Surrounding it was a broad wedge of dirt and rock that stretched from the wall to the middle of the Cut's floor. A slide! Just the way Mr. Fergueson had said it would look! William watched eagerly as scores of men scurried about, determining the best way to face this latest setback.

Lines of railroad track snaked along the floor of the Cut. More track down there than in Grand Central Station, William thought. More people too. Everywhere workers were attacking the earth with picks, shovels, and machines.

A dozen giant steam shovels scooped up dirt and rock and dropped them onto flatcars with such force that the sound roared up from the Cut. Spewing clouds of steam and coal dust, a locomotive began to haul out a full load of spoil. William followed it with his eyes. When he turned back to the steam shovel, a line of empty flatcars had already taken its place.

William wiped the sweat from his forehead. The tropical sun was already full in the sky. He wished he had brought a hat. He shaded his eyes with his hand and squinted into the sky. He had no idea what time it was.

Rightfully he should be able to stay as long as he wanted, he reasoned. Rightfully he should not have had to sneak out at all. But his parents seemed determined to make it difficult for him to do anything he considered important.

CHAPTER

THREE

William hurried to the front of the house and returned with a packing crate. He placed it under the
window and stepped up. Everything in his bedroom
was the way he had left it. The mound of clothes in
his bed looked like someone sleeping. He had done a
good job.

Sounds of banging from inside the house mixed with
the noise from the Cut. The smell of smoke drifted
out to him. He guessed his mother was working in
the kitchen.

William tugged at the edge of the screen, but it
wouldn't budge. He tried again with the same result.
He felt panic rising in him. He would have to think of

a phenomenal story if he had to go in through the front door.

He drew out his pocketknife and wiggled the longest blade between the window frame and the screen. Sweat dripping from his temples, he slowly pulled the blade out. The screen moved enough for him to get his fingers around it. He pulled, then jerked his hand away.

"Roosevelt's eyebrows," he hissed, looking at his thumb, where a long splinter was buried. He tried to pull it out with his teeth but couldn't get hold of the end. "Dumb bad luck." He took out his handkerchief and wrapped it around the thumb.

Again he tackled the screen with his knife. This time he managed to grab the screen and pull the bottom out enough to twist his upper body under it. He jumped up, flopped his stomach onto the sill, and crawled inside. He slipped off his muddy shoes and shoved them under the bed. His clothes looked as though he had slept in them, but that was nothing new. At least they weren't dirty.

Wiping his face on his sleeve, William went into the kitchen. The floor beneath him bounced on the wooden piles. As casually as he could, he leaned against the doorway and watched his mother kneeling in front of the range.

"Dad gone already?" he asked, his heart racing.

"Long since." She glanced up at him, then back

into the depths of the stove. "You must have been exhausted to sleep through all that noise. You'd have thought they'd build the living quarters farther away from that Cut."

"I think it's terrific," he said, relieved that she had not found him out.

"You would." Strands of dark hair, once part of the knot she had twisted on top of her head, formed a damp, matted frame around her face.

William grinned and picked at his splinter with his other thumb.

"I don't know why we even need a range," Mrs. Thomas said, fanning the coals. "It's hot enough to roast a pig without it. In a place like this, people should never cook."

"Is there anything for breakfast?" William asked.

"Just the bread and jam we bought before we got on the train yesterday. You'll have to fill up on that until we can order from the commissary."

William moved to the counter opposite the stove, cut a slice of bread, and spread it with jam. "Can I go to the Cut?" he asked, begging as he knew he would have if he had not yet been there. "I shouldn't be expected to stay away with it so close."

"It's close, all right," his mother retorted. "I heard the blasting all night."

"I ought to be able to spend at least part of my first day looking at it."

"It will still be there when your father has time to take you."

"No telling when that'll be."

"We should not have to go over this again," Mrs. Thomas said as she poked at the coals. A small cloud of smoke drifted into the room. "You agreed not to go anywhere dangerous alone, especially to that Cut. And you also agreed to help me unpack."

"It's not dangerous," William stated emphatically.

"You certainly sound sure of yourself. Perching on the edge of a huge chasm with no fence or anything else to prevent you from falling is most definitely dangerous. You are absolutely forbidden to go there alone. And you know it."

William folded the last of his bread and stuffed it into his mouth, thankful that he had not said more.

Mrs. Thomas slammed the door of the stove and stood up. "This is hopeless. We may have to eat coal for dinner."

CHAPTER

FOUR

William pulled a plate from a barrel of oily sawdust and wiped it with a linen towel. Cups and saucers rattled as he shoved the plate onto a shelf. His mother, lining the drawers of a cabinet in the living room, shot him a warning look. He gazed out the kitchen window, longing to be outside.

"Would you like help, lady?" someone called through the screen door of the veranda. "I can unpack crates, clean, or whatever you want. Only five cents an hour." On the steps stood a girl straight as a cultivated sapling, black as the soil of Panama. Her voice rose and fell in a strange melody.

She was tall, with thin arms. Her head was wrapped

in bright yellow cloth and topped with a straw hat. The screen masked the dark features of her face, but her eyes glowed like beacons announcing that something important was at hand.

William stared from the kitchen doorway, unable to take his eyes away. Back home in Maine, his father had often cared for Indians, and both parents had taught him that all God's children were important. But if people with skin as dark as freshly turned earth had entered his world before, William had never seen them.

Mrs. Thomas got up from the floor of the living room and wiped her hands on her apron. "What is your name?" she asked, walking to the door.

"Victoria, ma'am," the girl said, adding a slight curtsy. "The same as the last Queen of England—and Jamaica too." William stared, wondering if the curtsy was for his mother or if it somehow went with the name.

"Come in, Victoria. I am Mrs. Thomas." As Victoria came through the door, she caught it with her left hand so that it closed gently.

Mrs. Thomas pressed her hands together in front of her. William could tell that she was thinking. "If we don't have some help," she decided finally, "we may melt before these crates are unpacked. We will be glad to have you, until I have time to look for someone a little older."

"Yes, ma'am," Victoria answered with a hint of a frown.

"Five cents an hour sounds fine. Step into the living room, and I'll show you what to do." While William watched in fascination, his mother led Victoria to a row of small crates packed with faded red leather books. She lifted out a handful and carefully brushed away the wood shavings. "These books go in the bookcases in the dining room. Here, I'll show you."

Victoria followed Mrs. Thomas through the doorway that connected the living room and the dining room. Beneath the girl's long skirt, her bare feet padded across the floor, revealing light soles where, William supposed, the black had worn away.

"Stack them like this," Mrs. Thomas said as she settled the books on a shelf.

"Yes, ma'am," Victoria repeated as she and Mrs. Thomas returned to the living room. William watched as Victoria pulled a handful of books from a crate. She dusted them gently with her palm and stacked them on the floor. Then, rather than loading the books in her arms as he would have done, she slipped them onto her head, making a stack so high that her hands just reached the top. She turned and headed into the dining room, the books balanced skillfully on top of her head.

"How did she do that?" William asked in awe when she was gone.

"Amazing," his mother agreed. "Well, I'm going to put some of the clothes away," she explained as she turned toward the hall. "You need to get to work too."

William headed toward the kitchen, but in the doorway he paused to watch Victoria returning from the dining room, the hem of her faded skirt brushing the tops of her feet. When she saw him staring at her, she glared back.

William blushed and hurried into the kitchen. He hunched over the barrel and plunged his hand into the greasy sawdust. He pulled out a few dishes and slid them onto the shelf. A whistle from the Cut penetrated the walls. Before it was gone, another arrived to take its place. He picked at the splinter in his thumb. No doubt about it, this was shaping up to be a wasted day.

Her face pink from the heat, Mrs. Thomas came into the kitchen and looked at the shelves. "What have you been doing in here, William?"

William brushed his light brown hair off his forehead. "You've given me the worst job. This sawdust feels awful."

"Surely you remember choosing this job yourself." Mrs. Thomas had just dipped her hand into the barrel when there was a knock at the screen door. A rosy woman in a white dress and a large white hat was standing on the steps.

CHAPTER

F I V E

Mrs. Thomas set aside her apron and went to the door. The two women chatted briefly before moving to the wicker chairs on the veranda. A few minutes later, Mrs. Thomas called to William.

"Coming," he answered reluctantly. The only thing worse than missing out on the Cut would be listening to the boring talk of grown-ups. As William passed through the living room, he stole a glance at Victoria piling books on her head.

"Mrs. Roberts, this is our son, William," his mother said as he stepped onto the veranda.

"It's lovely to meet you," Mrs. Roberts said, the feather on her hat bobbing.

William bowed. "How do you do, Mrs. Roberts."

Mrs. Roberts took his hand and pulled him toward her. "Your mother tells me you're eleven, William."

"Yes, ma'am," he said, staring at the flecks of sawdust clinging to his shirt and squirming in her grasp.

"My oldest is a boy just your age. He is as interested in baseball as your mother says you are. I'll send him over, and you boys can get up a game." She sighed as she turned to Mrs. Thomas. "The boy plays well enough, but not as well as his father would like, I'm afraid."

"At least baseball is reasonably safe," Mrs. Thomas said to her guest.

William's eyes brightened. His mother's comment had given him an idea. "Does your boy get to go to the Cut?"

Mrs. Roberts grinned at William, patted his hand and released him. "I can guess what you're up to," she said, then she turned to Mrs. Thomas. "Things do happen in the Cut, but there's really no danger up here." William grinned as he savored this new bit of ammunition against his parents' rules. "They even take sightseers down there. Dynamite is the main hazard, but they're very careful with it."

Mrs. Thomas turned pale, but William added enthusiastically, "Six million pounds a year, that's how much they use in the Cut."

"William's always got some fact or another on the

tip of his tongue," his mother informed her guest wryly, "but he still has a lot to learn about some things." William frowned. His mother changed the subject. "Mrs. Roberts has brought us a nice dish for dinner, William."

"Just something to help until you can get going. We've all got to stick together, you know," Mrs. Roberts offered. For the first time, William saw the large platter covered with paper on the wicker table. "But now I'm going to take your mother away for a while," she continued. "It's just marvelous what you can do with these cottages if you use your imagination. You really must see what we've done with our place."

Mrs. Thomas looked around the veranda and chuckled at the mess. Crates and wood shavings mingled with the wicker furniture the ICC provided for each home.

Mrs. Roberts continued. "Before we came here, I'd never seen a house without plaster and wallpaper. Plants are the key—hide everything with plants. Of course, we have a large two-story. But count yourself lucky to have a house all to yourselves, even if it is an old one left over from the French fiasco."

"This was the vacancy closest to the hospital," Mrs. Thomas explained. "But it's a lot closer to the blasting than it is to anything else.

"You'll get used to that in time too," Mrs. Roberts assured her.

Mrs. Thomas stood. "I'll put this wonderful platter in the kitchen and get a hat."

"Don't forget an umbrella," Mrs. Roberts called.

"Honored to have met you," William said. He bowed to Mrs. Roberts and followed his mother out of the room.

Mrs. Thomas stood in front of the mirror in the hall and set a flat straw hat on her head. "I won't be away long. You keep working while I'm out, and we'll have things put away in no time."

"This would be a perfect time for me to go to the Cut," William suggested.

"Absolutely not!"

"You heard what Mrs. Roberts said. It's not dangerous at all," he protested.

"No. The rule stands."

William bit his lip.

"Now promise you'll stay and work, or I shall stay here and breathe down your neck while you unpack each and every dish."

"All right. I promise," he said irritably. "But I also protest."

His mother turned and hugged him. "A promise with protest is good enough for me."

When they returned to the living room, Mrs. Roberts was standing in the doorway. "I see you've already hired one of them," she said, nodding toward Victoria.

"Pardon?"

"You've already hired one of the coloreds."

"Victoria? Yes. We were lucky she found us," Mrs. Thomas said.

William held the screen door open. His mother squeezed his arm as she followed her guest out.

"Well, with almost no other help available, most people do hire them, but just let me tell you . . . ," Mrs. Roberts began as the two women drifted down the steps.

CHAPTER

S I X

William lifted the edge of the paper covering Mrs. Roberts's platter, peeked underneath, then tore off a bite of chicken and stuffed it into his mouth. He took another bite and stepped over to peer into the barrel he was unpacking. The injustice of his situation was as obvious as the sawdust in the barrel. Even when Mrs. Roberts had confirmed that going to the Cut was safe, his mother had not budged. He picked up a handful of sawdust and slammed it back into the barrel.

Taking a deep breath, he bent over and dug in. Gradually, his arms and hands became the neck and jaws of a steam shovel biting into the soil. Each dish became a mouthful of earth ripped away. He smiled.

With rhythm and force, he pushed his arms through the sawdust again.

"What should I do now?"

William gulped. He had no idea how long Victoria had been watching him. He guessed she was secretly laughing at him for imitating a steam shovel.

"I—I don't know," he stammered. "Mother didn't say."

"Should I help unpack dishes?"

"I guess so," he said, unable to force his eyes away from her.

Victoria searched the sawdust and pulled out a plate. She wiped it with the towel William handed her, then paused to straighten several stacks of dishes on the shelf before adding hers to one of them.

"You have more books than my whole schoolhouse back home," she said. Her voice slipped in and out of the words like a thrush's song.

"They're my mother's. She had them shipped here even though it cost a lot."

Victoria nodded and polished the rim of a cup. It was a long time before she spoke again. "Does she know that those books are going to ruin?"

"Ruin?" William exclaimed. He waited for her to explain, but instead, she placed the cup on the shelf and straightened the stacks again.

"How do you know they're going to ruin?" he asked finally.

"Everything ruins in Panama."

"That can't be true," William challenged.

Victoria sighed impatiently. "I worked for a woman who had some books with colored leather covers like those." William shifted his weight from one foot to the other, waiting for her to continue. "One day I was dusting and noticed a bit of green mold on some of them."

Victoria paused and swished her hand through the sawdust. William wondered if she was drawing out the story to tease him. "The next time I dusted them, more of the green was there. Soon it was all over the books. The lady had to pack them up and send them away so they wouldn't ruin completely."

Mold growing on books? She had to be wrong. Just as William opened his mouth to protest, the dishes began to clatter and the floor shook. Cups and plates crashed onto the floor. He held onto the range, and Victoria gripped the barrel as it bounced around the floor. The air crackled and vibrated with a roar that swelled and grew as though it would never stop.

CHAPTER

SEVEN

"Let's get out of here!" William darted out of the house and down the steps with Victoria just behind. Women and children poured out of other houses nearby. The boom ebbed, then burst forth again. "It's the Cut," he yelled as he grabbed the rail beside the front steps. "But it sounds like an earthquake."

At last, like an exhausted storm, the roar faded, giving way to frantic shouts and the rumble of machines.

"Come on. Let's see what's happened," William said, his voice shaking.

Victoria held back, her face as pale as driftwood. "It sounded like a huge slide. You may not like what you see."

But William was already gone, racing along the boardwalk, splatting through the grass and mud of the field. As he rushed to the edge, a woman ordered William to stay back. Her frightened gaze gripped him, and he slowed his pace, letting her get ahead, but he did not turn back. His heart raced. The field ahead was shorter than it had been that very morning. William inched his way forward and gazed down. A huge wedge of mud and rock had broken away and plunged downward, throwing the edge of the Cut back ten yards.

A man, buried to the waist, was screaming and ripping at the debris surrounding him. A dozen workers assaulted the rubble with shovels and picks or tore at boulders with their hands until at last they pulled him from the earth.

Near William a woman charged back and forth along the edge, wringing her hands. Close by, a group of women whispered among themselves, occasionally stealing glances into the Cut. William's stomach twisted nervously.

"It was just a matter of time until that cliff let go." Without looking around, he could tell it was Victoria.

"How can you say that?" he cried.

"That crack's been there for a week, getting wider every day. It was bound to let go soon and bury somebody."

William remembered the broad crack he had seen

that morning. "A crack means there's going to be a big slide?"

"Yes. Sometimes a sudden one like this, but usually a slow slide, like Cucaracha."

William followed her gaze across the Cut to the east. Cucaracha, "the Cockroach," was the oldest and most famous slide along the canal. How had he missed seeing it that morning, creeping down like a glacier? "But there haven't been many slides on this side of the Cut. Maybe this will be the last one," he said hopefully.

"And maybe they are a warning that digging this canal is wrong," Victoria said.

William stared at her. How could she possibly think that?

"I've seen several new slides lately, when I've come here to look home."

"To look home?" he asked, searching the top of the opposite cliff. "But there aren't any houses over there."

Victoria raised her arm and pointed across the mountains toward the sea. "There are lots of houses in Jamaica."

"Jamaica has got to be over five hundred miles from Panama. There's no way you could see it from here."

"I've seen it, all right. On days when the breeze blows the haze away, I can see it, out where the sky and sea meet, sparkling like a jewel."

"That's impossible!" he protested. "We steamed past

Jamaica on the way here. We couldn't see Panama from there. And that means you can't see Jamaica from here."

Victoria lifted her chin. "Maybe my eyes are better than yours."

"They can't be that good," said William. "You're right about one thing though. From the ship, Jamaica did look like an emerald floating on the sea."

"Like I said."

William shrugged and looked back down into the Cut. "They'll just have to dig it out again, like they do Cucaracha."

"If they can," Victoria said.

"They will," he said emphatically. "No matter how many times the sides let go, they'll dig it out. We're not like the French. They didn't have enough determination to build this canal. Or the equipment either. Their excavators were like toys compared to the steam shovels we use."

Victoria squinted at him. "There's a French excavator not far from where I once lived in the jungle," she said. "And it's huge."

"You mean there's a French excavator near Culebra?"

Victoria nodded as she turned back toward the houses.

"I've got to see it! Can you take me? How long would it take to get there?" he blurted out excitedly.

"Not long, but I don't have time to lead you to some

rusty old excavator. I've got to work for a living."

William hesitated, trying to think of a way to convince her. "I'll pay you what my mother is paying you," he said finally. "Five cents an hour. We'd have to leave at dawn though, and be back within two hours. Even then, I might get caught."

As she slid her feet through the grass, Victoria pursed her lips. "Tomorrow," she said finally. "We can go tomorrow at first light."

"Perfect," William said.

CHAPTER

E I G H T

Just as dawn split the darkness, William pushed out the screen and jumped. A shadow rounded the corner of the house. It was Victoria, her hat pulled down over her eyes. "You ready?" she whispered.

For the tenth time, William searched his mind and found plenty of reasons he should not go. He shoved them aside and nodded. "Sure."

When Victoria turned, her skirt moved, revealing a long knife half hidden in the folds.

"A machete," William said with awe. "May I hold it?"

Tentatively Victoria handed him the knife. "Be careful."

His fingers curled lightly around the wooden handle

and settled into grooves molded by the grasps of a thousand hands. A crescent of rust marked the end of the blade where the tip had broken off. "That's some knife," William declared, handing it back to her.

Victoria took the machete and led the way. Almost as soon as they were out of the village, they left the road, and the forest sprang up around them.

William slogged through the dimness. Plants crawled greedily over one another, intent on claiming the same spot. Many crept upward, winding round and round unsuspecting hosts to grow suspended in the air. Here and there huge trees, tall and stately, disappeared into the green canopy overhead in search of light.

Everywhere William stepped there was mud, sometimes in plain sight but often hidden under the fabric of the forest floor. Even when he kept his eyes on the ground, it grabbed his feet like powerful fingers.

"Go slower," he called, struggling to free a boot. He swatted at the insects in front of his face.

Victoria continued forward. "Keep moving," she warned.

But William moved cautiously, searching the ground for a firm spot. Suddenly two mosquitoes attacked his sweaty cheeks. He whacked his face and checked his hand. "I'll bet each of these monsters could drink a quart of blood," he said, pulling down his hat. He swatted at the bridge of his nose, and a mosquito tumbled down the front of his shirt.

Victoria looked back at him. "It's easier for them to bite if you stand still," she said.

William took a deep breath and struggled on.

The morning light was beginning to filter through the trees. Monkey howls and bird calls rose above the dull drone of millions of insects moving and chewing. The jungle, William decided, was almost as noisy as the Cut. He scratched a place under his right ear where he felt a mosquito bite swelling. "Maybe we should go back."

"We've come too far to go back. Watch that branch."

"Which branch?" William asked.

"There." Using the machete, she pushed back a leaf as big as her hand. On a branch sat a red frog the size of William's thumb. He leaned over to get a better view, then reached out to touch the creature. Instantly Victoria's arm shot forward to block his hand.

"It's poisonous," she said.

"I wasn't going to eat it."

Victoria nodded. "Poisonous to the touch."

A green snake slithered between them. William shuddered. "That's probably poisonous too."

"Yes," Victoria said. William slapped at the back of his neck as they moved on. A few moments later, Victoria started singing softly:

> *Muma me wan wuk,*
> *Muma me wan wuk,*

Muma me wan wuk.
Look how me muscle jump,
Look how me muscle jump.

She raised her machete to slice away an interfering plant, her voice gliding in and out of the notes.

Me wan fe dig yam hill,
Me wan fe dig yam hill,
Me wan fe dig yam hill.

William slopped through the mud to catch up with her. "That sounds like another language," he said.

"It's one of the languages of Jamaica. Many people use it when they talk or si—" Suddenly Victoria stopped. "Don't move," she whispered.

William's heart leaped into his throat, and he froze. She must have spotted something dangerous, he thought. Maybe a snake or poisonous spider dangling from a vine. Cautiously, he turned his head. A bright blue bird with a black mask stared silently at them from a nearby tree. A line of ants paraded down the trunk carrying bits of green. High in the canopy, leaves ruffled.

Her face stiff with fear, her eyes shifting, Victoria slowly lifted a string from around her neck and handed it to William. He stared at the strange necklace. "What's that for?" he whispered.

She raised a trembling hand to warn William not to speak and motioned for him to put it on. She touched an identical necklace around her neck to show that she had kept one for herself. He pulled the string over his head. Finally she seemed to relax. "That was close," she said, still whispering.

"I didn't see it, whatever it was," William said with alarm.

"It was a duppy," Victoria said. "Creeping through the forest like a shadow."

"This whole place is shadows," William responded, whacking at a diving mosquito. "And what's a duppy anyway?"

She pulled nervously at the brim of her hat. "A duppy is the spirit of a dead person roaming around loose."

William searched for signs that she was teasing, but her face was locked in fear.

"It's a spirit that's escaped from the grave," she explained, her voice shaking. "Once it's out, it haunts people."

"Like a ghost?" he asked. She nodded. He fingered the white objects on the string at his throat. "What are these things for?"

"Those are cowrie shells," she explained. "They help keep the duppy away. If you take them off, the duppy will get you for sure."

"The spirit will stay away from you if you wear

shells? That doesn't make sense."

She glowered at him from under the brim of her hat. "It's true," she said tersely.

Victoria was serious. She had walked through a jungle full of poisonous frogs, insects, and snakes, then cringed at a shadow. William wanted to laugh, but her fear held him back. "What will a duppy do to you?" he asked instead.

"Follow you home. Bother you and your house. Make you sick. Make you lose your job. Duppies can make everything go wrong."

"I don't think I believe in these spirits," he said, trying to be polite.

"If one of them follows you home, it doesn't matter whether you believe in it or not."

William lifted the string to pull it off. To their left, the bushes stirred. He looked around but saw nothing to explain the movement. Victoria gave him a warning glare, and he dropped the string. After a few moments, she crept forward, her eyes scanning the forest.

CHAPTER

N I N E

Before long, Victoria and William reached a small clearing slashed by the fall of an enormous tree. The tree's sheared roots, which stood three times as high as William, were draped with jungle greenery and bathed in sunlight. Scattered around the rotting tree lay smaller trunks. Nearby sat the cause of the destruction—a machine that had gnawed at the forest floor decades ago and weakened the hold of the tree's roots. Green vines covered it now like moss on a stone.

"There's the tiny French excavator," Victoria said teasingly. "The jungle's swallowed it like a toad swallows a fly."

William searched the clearing. At last he spotted the huge machine. "Beautiful. Absolutely beautiful," he said as he walked toward it.

A long belt of buckets sloped from the middle of the excavator to the forest floor. A giant crane crossed the bucket assembly and stretched upward. Foliage draped everywhere. Together the two arms of the excavator looked like the jaws of a green monster ready to chew up the jungle.

Here and there patches of rust showed through the greenery like bright tropical flowers. William touched a spot and grinned at the red-orange grains of rust that came off on his fingers. "This could have been here twenty-five years, just waiting for us to find it."

In his mind William could see the machine move. He could hear the buckets scrape and grind against the earth, the belt rattle as its containers moved skyward, and the soil thud onto a waiting flatcar. Smells of musty soil, hot metal, steam, and coal swirled around him. "These excavators were nowhere as good as our steam shovels are, and they couldn't handle rocks for anything," he explained. He turned to Victoria. Her eyes were searching the forest, and she was not paying attention.

William looked back at the crane. He had to climb it. He had to reach the highest point of the excavator. He put one foot onto the bucket assembly, then care- fully placed the other behind it. Driven by the image of himself at the top, William crept upward. Sometimes his toes perched on the vines, sometimes they found holds in the belt.

When William reached the spot where the bucket assembly crossed the crane, he realized it was higher than it looked from the ground. Gripping the lattice in front of him, he swung one leg up, then the other. Carefully he crawled out to the end of the crane and sat down. With one hand he held on. With the other he doffed his hat to the world.

The sun pounded his head, and the breeze brushed the top of the crane. From his perch William could see that a broad area of young trees separated the clearing where the excavator sat from the rest of the jungle. These trees, he decided, must have grown up where French machines had cut away the forest many years before. The Americans had obviously abandoned this part of the old canal.

William breathed deeply, and again the excavator came alive. The buckets on the assembly below him rattled to a stop, and the crane where he sat swung toward a new piece of earth. A train loaded with soil rumbled away into the distance. How could the French have given up? How could they have abandoned their glorious machines to the jungle?

"Victoria," he shouted. "Look at me!"

"You're pretty stupid. You'll probably break your neck, and before you've paid me a cent," she yelled up to him. William was sure he could see her smile.

Testing each toehold, he slowly made his way to the ground and then stepped to the side of the platform. As he reached out to part the vines, Victoria stopped him for the second time that day.

"What are you doing?"

"I want to go in."

"It's better just to look. Something may live there. Maybe a snake. Maybe spiders."

William jerked his hand away. It had not occurred to him that more than plants could have claimed the excavator. Victoria pierced the foliage with the blade of the machete and pulled back a narrow curtain of rich green.

"Look. Don't touch," she warned again.

William bent forward and peered inside. "It's so dark I can't see very well." Along the floor of the platform, shriveled tendrils lay in heaps. He supposed they had climbed along the wheel assembly and levers until others grew over them and blocked their light.

"There's nothing here except dead vines," William said. But as he spoke, a mound of leaves moved and a furry white face appeared. Two shiny dark eyes and a downturned mouth scowled out at him. "A monkey," William whispered.

Black fur on the top of its head and on its body made the monkey look like it was wearing a suit and matching cap. A smaller monkey, clinging to the shoulders of the first, stared crossly at him.

"Two monkeys," he corrected himself. "Must be a mother and a baby." Victoria looked into the opening and nodded.

The mother reached up, grabbed a lever draped in leaves, and bared her teeth. "Cheeeeeeee!" She shrieked so loudly that William and Victoria jumped back. "Cheeeeeeee," she screamed again as she sprang to the top of the lever. Then, with the baby holding on, she scampered up the vines, off the excavator, and into the branches of a nearby tree, screeching all the while.

William put his hands over his ears and laughed. "Boy, she's loud." From the safety of the tree, the mother continued to shriek, as though scolding William and Victoria for trespassing.

"Look. There," Victoria said, pointing. Another monkey, larger than the mother and more squarely built, glared at them from a nearby tree. It squatted on a branch with its hands on its hips. The ridge above its eyes moved angrily, and the white ruffs on the sides of its face flared. For a moment it stared, then it shook the tree and screeched. "Chee, chee, chee, cheeeee!"

As though obeying a summons, two more animals appeared and added their screams. Still others followed until the trees were dotted with screeching monkeys.

"They're angry!" Victoria said.

William nodded. "There must be a dozen of them. I don't know anything about monkeys, but it looks to me like they are going to attack us. Do you think they could hurt us?"

"Well, I've got a machete," Victoria said, holding up the knife in front of her, "and I'm ready if th— Look out!"

CHAPTER

T E N

A round, green fruit sailed toward William's chest.
Just in time, he jumped aside. The fruit hit the ground
and split open, spilling yellow pulp onto the ground.
The monkey screeched and threw another piece of
fruit. Using its tail and one hand, a second monkey
moved through the branches, pulled something from
the tree, and threw it.

The large monkey swung down from the top of the
tree until it sat just above them, eyeing William. Like
an expert, it aimed and threw. Again William tried to
dodge the missile, but this time it hit his shoulder and
bounced off.

"Ow!" That hurt," he shouted, rubbing the shoulder.

"They're serious! What should we do?" He peered nervously into the trees.

Three more monkeys screeched and swung lower in the trees. Victoria, eyes wide and jaw set, raised the machete and jumped forward with a shout. The monkeys froze where they were. Victoria and William looked at each other.

"Maybe that's it. Maybe we have to act fierce," Victoria said.

"Maybe." William jumped up and down, flapping his arms. "Cheeeeee!" he screamed, trying to echo the threatening sounds of the monkeys. "Cheeeeeeeee, cheeeeeee!" The monkeys continued to stare.

"It's working!" she shouted, then took up the act.

William screamed again, trying to make his voice as loud and as full as possible.

The monkeys shrieked back at them.

Screeching, William and Victoria flapped their arms wildly and jumped forward a few steps.

Two overgrown adversaries were too much for the leader. He scowled at them and retreated to the top of the tree, the others right behind. The animals stopped, turned, and stared at the noisy humans. Then they withdrew nonchalantly into distant trees. William made a few exaggerated leaps to make sure the monkeys stayed away.

Victoria erupted with laughter. "You look awfully funny." William laughed too, and they gave in to their hilarity, tears of relief coating their cheeks.

"That monkey imitation sure worked," Victoria said at last.

William wiped his cheek with a dirty hand. "They were surprised."

"And scared! But we'd better go before they realize we're harmless and come back."

"Just a minute," William said. "I want to get a souvenir from the excavator."

"A souvenir?"

"Sure." He walked back to the bucket assembly at the front of the steam shovel. Here and there he shook the belt, searching for something that would give way. He soon found a rusty bolt, loose after years in the rain forest. With his thumb and forefinger, he freed the nut underneath and held the two treasures in his stained palm. "Aren't they terrific?" he asked, returning to Victoria.

"Maybe to some people," Victoria said, shaking her head.

William stuffed the nut and bolt deep into his pocket. "I wish there were some shorter way to get back. Fighting that mud is harder than walking through six feet of snow."

Victoria's eyes widened. "Snow? You've been in snow?"

"Sure. Tons of it. Where I come from, it snows all winter long. And sometimes half of the spring."

"It never snows in Panama. Or in Jamaica either," she said. She turned and pointed. "There's a railroad near here. We can follow the tracks right back to Culebra if you want."

"You mean we could have walked all this way along a railroad bed?"

She nodded.

"Why in the world didn't we come that way?"

"We would have passed right through Culebra, and people would have seen us for sure."

"And probably stopped us," William concluded. "Well, it doesn't matter anymore. It must be hours since we left. I couldn't possibly get into more trouble than I'm in already."

Victoria shrugged and led the way along a path with ruts worn deep by use and rain. William concentrated on the slick clay beneath his feet. At first he walked above the ruts, sliding several times and almost falling. Finally he decided to walk inside them. The mud and slime coated his stockings, but at least the level bottom kept him from slipping. When he was on firmer ground, he took the nut and bolt out of his pocket and looked at them again. "What a prize!"

"You're a strange one, Snowman, acting like a rusty bolt is a treasure."

William chuckled at the name. With sweat sliding off his face and insects attacking him, he didn't feel much like a snowman. And as for being strange, surely everybody would consider a rusty bolt from one of the canal's old excavators a valuable souvenir. Then he remembered the encounter with the duppy and the strings of shells they were wearing around their necks. "You're pretty strange yourself," he said with a grin.

CHAPTER

ELEVEN

"**Y**ou could have been killed out there!" William's mother fumed as she paced back and forth in the dining room.

William sat at the table, his face in his hands. "Whenever we came near anything dangerous, she warned me," he said.

"How polite of her, dear." Bitterness laced his mother's words. "So comforting for you to know the cause of your death before it happens."

William's father sat across from him, drumming his fingers on the table. "If a mosquito with the malaria parasite bit you, you could be in real trouble."

Mrs. Thomas raised an eyebrow. "*A* mosquito didn't

bite him. He has obviously been attacked by an army of them."

William stared at the welts on his hands. "I had to do something. You want to keep me penned up here forever."

"There is a difference between 'doing something' and sneaking into the jungle where the mosquitoes bore into you like bullets from a Gatling gun," his mother replied.

William smiled inwardly. The insects *had* seemed like bullets—bullets that could change direction when he tried to fend them off.

"Your mother says you're invited to play baseball with that nice Bud Roberts anytime you want," his father said. "Why couldn't you have done that instead? That's 'something.'"

William raised his head. "I can play baseball back home. The jungle is what Panama's all about," he said, his eyes bright.

Mrs. Thomas looked at William in disbelief. "What about the canal? Don't they call it 'the eighth wonder of the world?'"

"Of course," William said passionately as he juggled the inconsistency. "Panama *is* the canal. But it's the jungle too. That French excavator was just standing there, rusty, with vines climbing all over it. Insects were flying around everywhere, and it was hot and humid. It was wonderful!"

"It sounds awful—and dangerous too," Mrs. Thomas remarked.

"It wasn't dangerous!" William protested. "We were very close to the rail line. Victoria knew exactly where we were the whole time."

"I don't know that, and neither do you. You are both just children."

The bites on William's face were an angry red. "You've got to stop treating me like a baby. You won't let me look at the Cut by myself, and some of the water boys who work down there aren't even as old as I am."

"That is beside the point," his father said. "Charging into the jungle with your little friend was extremely irresponsible."

Mrs. Thomas leaned toward William. "You did something that could have cost us all dearly." Her soft voice made him stiffen. "And because of that, you shall not leave this house for a week."

"A week!" William shot up from his chair so quickly that it almost fell over.

"A week," his father echoed.

"That's unfair," William said, doing his best to keep his voice steady and hold back his tears.

"It's quite fair," his mother said firmly, "especially since you had to know that going into the jungle was foolhardy and against the rules."

"There are so many rules in this house that I might

as well not even *try* to remember them all."

"Well you'd better remember this one," his father stated firmly, "because if we catch you going into the jungle again, you won't get out of your room until you're grown."

And that was that.

The screen bulged as a mosquito the size of William's hand scraped against it. At any moment the giant insect would break through and feed upon him.

The scratch came again. William opened his eyes and looked around. Against the light from the window, William saw Victoria's head at the base of the screen. Her scratching had shaped the end of his dream.

When he slid out of bed, his foot crunched something. He knew he had cracked the shell of one of the large roachlike beetles that searched the house for food and adventure. He scanned the floor before he scooted to the window.

"First light, Snowman."

In the crisis with his parents, he had forgotten their decision to go to the Cut at dawn the next day. "I can't go, Victoria. I'm in deep trouble, and my parents won't let me out of the house for a week."

"Truly?"

William nodded. "My punishment for going into the jungle."

Except for a crescent of light reflected by a cheek-bone, Victoria's face was hidden in darkness. "Doing nothing for a week doesn't sound like a punishment to me, Snowman. It sounds like a holiday."

"But I can't see the Cut for a whole week. And I can never go into the jungle again."

"Are you sure your famous Cut will be there when you get out?" Victoria teased. "There was another slide yesterday, behind the center of the village. That's two slides on this side in two days. The whole village will probably be at the bottom of the Cut by the time you get out."

William frowned, angry that he could not see the slide and annoyed that he had managed to be jailed before he had even investigated the village. "Don't worry. The Cut will still be there, and it will be deeper too. But in the meantime, I'll probably go crazy." His face brightened with an idea. "Do you think you could visit me sometime?"

"Maybe," she said.

"Thanks. If the smoke clears around here, I hope to talk my parents into letting me out early."

Five days later William heard Victoria scratch on the screen again. He was sitting on his bed, reading. He checked the floor for insects, then crept to the window.

"I was afraid you wouldn't come back," he whispered.

"I was here the day before yesterday, just before

noon. You must have been out having a good time."

William shook his head. "My parents aren't as angry at me as they were, but they've barely let me out of my room, except to work. That was the day I was scrubbing out the dry room. My mother stores practically all of our clothing in there to keep it from getting mildewed. She made me take out everything and wash the whole place with something smelly."

"That sounds like fierce punishment," Victoria teased.

"It wasn't as bad as drinking quinine. Because of all those mosquito bites, they're making me take it, even though I'm not the least bit sick. It's the worst-tasting stuff in the world."

"I know," she said. "My father's been taking it." She lifted the basket she was holding and put it on her head.

William searched for something else to say. He didn't want her to leave. "Where will you go now?" he asked.

"To the public market to buy fruit for a lady, then back to wash her floors. After that, I'll look for more work—whatever I can get. It's hard to find, because lots of people don't like to hire someone so young."

At first William was envious. Working for pay sounded grown-up and exciting. Then he thought about the backbreaking job of cleaning the dry room and was glad that he didn't have to work that hard every day.

"I almost forgot," he said. "A miracle has happened! My parents have decided to start letting me go to the Cut once my week is up!"

"But you've already been there—the other day, after the slide. Weren't you supposed to?"

William shook his head.

"In that case it sounds like a miracle all right. How did you talk them into it?"

"I didn't! Colonel Gaillard, the man who heads the work in the Cut, did! He must be my guardian angel! One day when he wasn't feeling well, he went to the hospital. Lucky for me, my father treated him," William explained. "When they were finished, he asked Father all about himself and his family, and the conversation worked around to my wanting to spend time at the Cut.

"Colonel Gaillard said there was no reason to keep me from going there. He walks along it every day himself, he said, and the riskiest thing is tripping over American sightseers!"

"The jungle is dangerous, and the Cut is safe?!" Victoria said in disbelief.

"Well, from above, anyway," William said. "The fine fellow even took Father to the rim to point out how safe it is, and he promised Father a steak dinner at the Tivoli Hotel in Ancon for every time I fell in! Father laughed when he told Mother the story, but I guess it made them think.

"I've told them a hundred times that looking at the Cut isn't dangerous, and they wouldn't listen. But a few words from Colonel Gaillard, and they're convinced to give me a chance! My parents are hard to understand sometimes."

"Mine too," said Victoria. "It must be part of the job."

William nodded. "So starting next week, I get to go every day from noon to one o'clock," he explained. "If the machines start working or if it rains, I have to come home. And if I mess up once, I don't get to go again—ever.

"But what do you say?" William added excitedly. "How about meeting me the day after tomorrow at the place where we saw the slide that first day?"

Victoria's face grew serious. "I'll be there if I can. Things move awfully fast sometimes." She adjusted the basket on her head. "See you later," she said as she ducked behind the window frame and disappeared.

CHAPTER

TWELVE

Two days later, at exactly twelve noon, William headed for the Cut. The humid air made him feel as if he were wading through an ocean of tepid water. He hoped the rain would hold off until one o'clock.

When he saw Victoria waiting for him, he broke into a run. "You came!" he shouted.

"Of course," Victoria said behind a smile.

Because of the dinner break, the steam shovels on the floor of the Cut stood silent and still. But men were still at work stuffing dynamite into the wedge of earth that had plunged down the week before. William looked down at the scene. "They've gotten out a lot of the dirt from the slides already."

"Yes, but there will probably be another one before they get these cleared."

William was about to protest when Victoria looked beyond the Cut and spoke again. "Jamaica's hard to see with the clouds coming in."

William squinted toward the horizon. "Not that again. I can't even see the ocean from here, much less an island in it. The mountains block the view."

Victoria sighed impatiently and pointed. "Look over the top of that ridge."

William tried, but all he could see was a sky littered with clouds and interrupted by green mountain peaks. Then, just as he looked away, he thought he caught a glimpse of a green island shining in a blue sea. But when he glanced back, it had vanished behind a racing cloud.

"For a second I thought I saw it." Then he frowned. "But I couldn't have."

"You couldn't see the French excavator at first either, and it was right in front of you."

William laughed as he remembered the way the jungle had seemed to swallow the great machine. "That's true," he admitted.

William felt several raindrops, and a moment later the clouds broke open. The rain gushed down, collecting in pools on the saturated soil and rushing down the steep slopes of the Cut. "I'm not going to stand here and watch the water pour into that ditch, Snowman.

See you tomorrow, if I can," Victoria shouted as she ran toward the road.

William waved. He did not want to leave, but he knew his parents would forbid him to return if he stayed. So as the rain masked the Cut, he reluctantly turned and headed home.

The next morning William and his mother sat on the veranda. Once again rain poured down in thick sheets, pounding the roof hard enough to drown out sounds from the Cut. The rainy season was in full force. William wondered how much water the soil could absorb before more slides would occur.

Perched on the arm of his chair, Mrs. Thomas held her son's hand on her lap and teased the inflamed skin of his thumb with a needle. "If you had told me about this splinter when you first got it, it wouldn't be so awful."

William rubbed his clammy forehead with his free hand and leaned around his mother to see what she was doing.

"Don't look," she warned. "That will just make it worse." William nodded. "Mrs. Roberts said her son and his friends would come by this morning. Why don't you play with them? You would have a wonderful time."

William wiggled. "But then I'll miss my one chance all day to see the Cut. Of course, there would be no problem if you would let me go at a different time—and maybe for longer?"

His mother tightened her grip and twisted her body to block his view. She broke the skin with the needle.

"Ow!" he yelled, certain that she was being rougher than necessary. "I'm not made of wood, you know."

"If you were, the splinter could stay there quite happily." She caught the splinter with the needle and pulled, but only the tip came away.

"What are you doing?" he shouted. He placed the elbow of his free arm on his knee and laid his forehead in his sweaty palm.

"Trying to make sure that you do not get an infection. You may think Panama is a paradise, but it's loaded with germs, and even small wounds can lead to trouble." She teased open a bit more skin, hooked the splinter, and pulled.

"Mother," William moaned.

"All done," she said, releasing his arm.

William looked at the thumb. "Gosh, Mother, you left a crater."

"About the size of the Cut," she joked. "Now we'll wash it with soap and water and put on some gauze to keep the wound clean."

William followed his mother into the kitchen. She ran a basin of water and handed him a cake of soap. "How did you get this anyway?" she asked as he soaped his hand, grimacing.

"I—I don't remember. You know how you sometimes get a splinter and don't know how?" He hoped she would attribute his red face to the sting of the soap. He rinsed his hand and stared at the thumb.

"Probably on one of the crates when we unpacked," she said as she went off to search for the gauze.

"Probably," William agreed.

The rain ended as suddenly as it had begun, and the hot sun sent columns of steam rising from the ground. When William leaned forward in his chair, his shirt stuck to his back. The sound of clanging steam shovels reached his ears, and he felt envious as he imagined the workers and their machinery so near.

Around the curve in the road, three boys appeared. Each wore a cap and carried a glove. One boy, a fringe of blond hair gleaming under the brim of his cap, looked more solid and muscular than the others. His gloved hand jabbed the air in front of him, and his feet shuffled like a boxer's. He glanced toward the Thomas house, then said something to a boy swinging a bat at his side. The boy with the bat tilted his hat back on his head and nodded. Even from the veranda, William could see that he had a red, sunburned face and a white nose where the skin had peeled away.

A tall, thin boy walked behind the first two. As he tossed a baseball into the air with his right hand, he rocked to the left. With the next step, he rocked to the right and caught the baseball with his other hand.

Shocks of red hair poked out from under his hat.

"That's Bud and his friends," Mrs. Thomas said, walking to the screen door.

The boys laughed so loud that William could hear one of them snort. He kicked at the chair with his heel and wished they hadn't come.

CHAPTER

THIRTEEN

By the time the boys clattered up the steps, they were
on their best behavior. The tall boy held open the
screen door for the others to enter. The three filed inside and took off their caps.

"Nice to see you, Bud," William's mother said to the
boxer.

"Hello, Mrs. Thomas," he replied before turning to
William. "I'm Bud Roberts. This is Hamilton Miller.
And that's Jeremy Barnes." He jabbed his thumb at
the boy with the ball. They both nodded.

"Hello," William said.

"We were about to play a little baseball and were
wondering if you would like to play."

William searched for an excuse. He couldn't bear to miss his measly hour at the Cut. "I don't have my glove. I think it's still packed away somewhere. Or, uh, uh, maybe I forgot to bring it."

Bud pursed his lips. Jeremy glanced at Hamilton, then looked away. Hamilton shrugged.

"Your glove is in the trunk at the foot of your bed," William's mother offered. "I'm sure I saw it there yesterday. Go have some fun, dear."

William grimaced. "Maybe we could play tomorrow morning," he added hastily, afraid he was making the wrong impression. "Not so close to noon. Or I might even be able to find my glove by this afternoon."

Bud shrugged. "I can't this afternoon."

Mrs. Thomas smiled. "Then how about a glass of lemonade before you go?" For the first time, William noticed a pitcher of lemonade and some glasses on the table in the corner. His mother must have been planning this all along. The boys tumbled into chairs while William helped his mother.

"What brought your family to Culebra, Hamilton?" she asked, handing a full glass to William.

Hamilton scratched his sunburned forehead. "My father has a job in the payroll office, dishing out money. He doesn't get to the Cut like Bud's and Jeremy's fathers. Jeremy's dad supervises the dynamite operations in this end of the Cut."

"Gosh," William said, his interest awakened. He

offered Jeremy the first glass, but the boy shook his head shyly and looked at the floor.

"You probably know that my dad's an engineer on a steam shovel down there," Bud said.

William's face beamed with admiration as he presented the glass of lemonade to Bud. "Really? Mother didn't tell me."

Bud lifted his chin, conscious of the high status of his father's occupation. "Uh huh. He's digging in the Cut on the other side of the village. Some days when we play baseball, he even stops by at noon to toss a few. Then he and I walk home to dinner together."

"Is your dad going to pitch to you today?" William asked, handing Hamilton some lemonade. The possibility of meeting a steam-shovel operator dangled before him.

Bud nodded. "Sure is."

"We'd better be going," Jeremy said softly, rubbing the ball back and forth in his glove.

"Hold on a minute," William blurted. "I—I'll see if I can find my glove."

The boys exchanged looks. "Whatever you say," Hamilton offered.

William bounded out of the room. Moments later he returned with his cap and glove. "It was in my trunk, just like you said, Mother."

"See you after noon then," his mother said as the boys clattered out the door.

William followed them along the boardwalk and onto the road. Bright, hot sunlight surrounded them, and he could feel drops of moisture collecting on his skin like insects on a light bulb. Rumbles, clatters, and clangs chased dust, soot, and steam out of the Cut, which William glimpsed between the houses. How could these boys saunter by without dashing to the edge?

As they ambled down the road, Bud started shuffling back and forth, jabbing the air. Hamilton and Jeremy giggled. Bud shuffled more wildly, punching high and low until the two boys laughed. Bud glanced back at William and grinned. William smiled faintly. He felt too new to understand the humor, but he knew he wanted to be friends with the steam-shovel operator's burly son.

Tall, slender palm trees graced the road into the center of Culebra. Along the road, the boys passed a man with a tank strapped to his back. He was spraying oil in a water-filled ditch so that mosquito larvae could not survive there.

Behind the palms stood scattered houses, their screened verandas held solidly and neatly in place by white framing. Some were bungalows like William's, but most were two-story buildings for two or more families. None of the houses touched the ground. Instead they stood on wooden posts. Underneath, protected from the sun, fuzzy carpets of green mold thrived.

William shuddered as he thought of the snakes and insects lurking there.

Hamilton turned to William. The new skin on his nose glistened in the sunlight. "This is all gold housing. But you probably know that already."

William shook his head. "Not really." William knew that the ICC had two different payroll systems. American employees were paid in gold currency, and almost everyone else got wages in silver. William had never quite understood what that meant.

"Only Americans live in the housing for gold employees," Bud explained. "The coloreds are silver. Most of their kind live out in the bush or in Panama City or Colón and come in on the labor trains every day." Bud pointed to a large cottage with a tangle of plants on the veranda. "That's where I live. Steamshovel operators always get the best houses," he said proudly.

William nodded. That made perfect sense to him.

The four boys rounded a curve and arrived at the village center. Children, women, and men of every color and description walked along the street, flowing in and out of the buildings.

"Roosevelt's knickers!" William gasped as he gazed at the opposite side of the street. A woman of rich, burnished brown carried a large cloth bundle on her head. A black canal policeman chatted with a short, dark-haired man with almond-shaped eyes. On a nearby corner, a woman with skin the shade of egg shells hid her face under a wide-brimmed hat. "There must be someone from every country in the world on this street!"

CHAPTER

FOURTEEN

"Yeah. Too many colored people! My dad says they clog up the works everywhere," Bud said.

Absorbed in watching the people, William did not hear. The group moved onto the boardwalk so that a cart could pass on the road.

Hamilton pointed to a long building. "There's the commissary. And next to it are the bachelors' quarters, for some of the single men working here." Two wings of a large, screened building jutted out almost to the road. "ICC headquarters is on down the road a piece."

As Hamilton spoke, a woman who had left the commissary headed along the boardwalk toward the boys.

On her head she carried a basket that she held in place with one hand. With the other hand she led a small boy. Her dark face and eyes reminded William of Victoria.

Within a few feet of the boys, the pair stepped off the boardwalk onto the wet grass and stopped. Bud and the others walked past them, but William politely stepped off the boardwalk and, shifting uneasily from one foot to another, waited for the woman to pass.

At first she looked at the ground, but when William did not move, she lifted her eyes to look at his face. Slowly she narrowed her eyes, and William looked away, confused.

"Hey, William," Hamilton called. "Come on."

William hurried after the others.

"Why did you do that?" Bud challenged.

"Well, uh," William stammered, wondering if these boys had learned different manners.

"Gold never gets off for silver. No matter what," Bud stated emphatically.

William blushed. This place sure had strict rules.

In front of the commissary, William saw a sign that read "Gold-roll Employees," with an arrow pointing to the left. Underneath were the words "Silver-roll Employees," with an arrow pointing to the right. Like light passing through a prism, people of light and dark hues separated in front of the building and vanished through different doors.

"That's the YMCA clubhouse," Bud said as he nodded toward the large building next to the bachelors'
quarters. "Most single guys spend their free time
there, reading the papers, playing games. Carl and
Howard are supposed to meet us in front."

"The last slide happened behind the YMCA!"
William said, trying to see between the buildings.

"The other guys are already here," Jeremy said. Two
boys were leaning against the gazebo on the YMCA's
lawn. "Carl! Catch," he shouted as he released a
long throw.

As one of them snagged the ball, the two boys
headed toward the others. "You must be William. I'm
Howard, Jeremy's brother," said a boy with red hair
who was almost as tall as Jeremy.

"And I'm Carl," said a short, skinny boy wearing a
cap that was too small for his head. He shook hands
with William, then flipped the ball to Howard.

William hardly noticed the introductions. Not fifty
yards away, steam and smoke floated like a gray banner
over the Cut. None of the other boys seemed to care
that the Cut was there.

Hamilton handed the bat to Jeremy, who took a few
practice swings, his arms so long that the bat looked as
if it might be a part of them. Bud started across the
road toward a playing field tucked among some
houses. "It's my turn to pitch."

"You always pitch," Carl complained.

"It's my turn anyway," Bud said. "William, you play second base."

"Hey, Bud. Catch," Howard shouted. He threw the ball across the road to Bud, lobbing it over the head of a black woman who frowned in reply.

William stayed where he was. He knew he could not play until he'd seen the Cut. "Say," he shouted to the others. "I've got to go over to the Cut. I've never seen it from here."

Bud turned and tossed the ball to Hamilton, who quickly flipped it back again. "Why didn't you say so before? Come on, fellows."

"Sure. Let's go," the others called, eager to show the new boy the sights. As Bud led them toward the canal, the irregular mouth of the Cut opened before them.

CHAPTER

FIFTEEN

Propelled by the sight below, William strode along the edge while the others crowded around him. Compared with the stretch near his house, twice as many men labored around twice as many steam shovels. Far to the left hung a row of ladders that workers used to climb in and out of the Cut.

Carl nudged Hamilton with his elbow. "Hey! There's the Yellow Peril!" Turning to William he explained, "That's what the colonel calls his observation car. Couldn't have timed it better if we'd had an appointment."

Along the main track in the Cut below, they watched a bright yellow railway car approaching. It looked like a giant automobile with a cowcatcher on the front. The car came to a stop, and a tiny figure dressed in a dark suit got out.

"There's Colonel George Washington Goethals himself," Bud proclaimed.

William was jubilant. "It *is* him!"

The boys watched in awe as the director of the entire canal project took off his jacket and slung it over his shoulder, then walked over to talk to a group of workers and look over their machines. Several minutes later the colonel climbed back aboard, and the yellow car traveled further down the Cut.

"It's at least 115 down there in Hell's Gorge, but he's with the rest of them, baking like a turkey at Thanksgiving," Jeremy said.

"You'll see Colonel Goethals a lot, really," Carl told William, trying to sound casual. "Likes to keep up with how the digging is going, especially here in the Cut." Nevertheless, the boys watched in respectful silence until the Yellow Peril was out of sight.

Setting off again, the boys soon came to the sight of a recent slide. A ramp of soil and boulders started halfway down the bank and ran far onto the floor of the Cut. At the base of the ramp, men broke up the rock, and steam shovels scooped it up, determined to correct nature's mistake. "All that's from the slide," Bud said. "Every time it happens, the colonel says, 'Dig it out.'"

Not far below them, a crew of dark-skinned men dug their shovels into wet clay and heaved it into the wide jaws of a steam shovel. When it was full, the machine's dipper dropped the clay onto a waiting car, where it flattened and spread like a giant spoonful of pudding.

As the crew began digging again, one man turned over his shovel and tapped the blade until the contents fell into the jaws. When he straightened up, he saw the boys and raised his shovel in salute.

Thrilled that someone who worked in the Cut had noticed them, William waved back wildly.

"What are you doing?" Bud shouted.

"Waving," William said. "Didn't you see that man raise his shovel at us?"

"You're not supposed to wave at coloreds."

"What?" William asked. Bud wasn't making any sense.

"I told you before, whites don't have anything to do with coloreds." Bud pounded the ball into his glove.

"But they're practically building the whole canal! How can you keep from having anything to do with them?"

"You just do, that's all."

Carl glanced sympathetically at William.

"The races don't mix," Hamilton explained.

"Housing, mess halls, and everything else are separate," Howard added.

"Hey! We've been here long enough," Jeremy said. "Let's play."

As the boys turned from the Cut, Bud and Jeremy began tossing the ball in a high arc over the head of the others. Carl and Howard rushed back and forth between them, leaping up to try to catch the ball. Jeremy threw it wide, and Carl jumped to the side and nabbed it. Then he and Howard tossed the ball back and forth, keeping it away from the other two. By the time the boys crossed the road to the playing field, they were laughing and joking.

The incident had passed for the others, but William was still confused and embarrassed. He sure was getting off on the wrong foot with Bud, but his new friend was sounding like some sort of a policeman. Bud must never have met anyone like Victoria, William decided. Otherwise he wouldn't think the way he did.

Bud blasted two fastballs low and inside. Jeremy fanned them. Bud is good, William thought. "Great pitching," he yelled.

On a slow third pitch, Jeremy's bat connected. The ball skated by second base and into the outfield. William tore after it. When the ball hit a low spot where rain had collected, it stopped. William scooped it up and blasted it straight to Hamilton at first base.

"What an arm!" Carl shouted as Hamilton threw it back to the pitcher's mound.

"Thanks," William called back. Bud kicked at the ground in front of him.

When William came up to bat, he watched two pitches, fouled another, then sent the fourth deep into the outfield, ricocheting off the veranda of the nearest house. As William rounded third, Carl shouted, "You've got your work cut out for you now, Roberts."

"Shut up," Bud snarled. He threw so high and hard to third that the ball almost hit Carl in the head.

A whistle bellowed out of the Cut. Soon another joined it. A few minutes later, a man solid and rectangular like Bud walked onto the field.

"Hello, Dad," Bud said as the man joined him at the pitcher's mound. The man snatched Bud's cap and gave his son's head a firm rub with the knuckles.

Bud reddened as he leaped for his cap, which the man held high above the boy's head. "Hey, Dad! Don't!" he pleaded. Mr. Roberts plopped the cap back on his son's head.

"This is William Thomas," Hamilton said as the boys gathered around Mr. Roberts.

Mr. Roberts extended an arm as large as a tree trunk. "How do you do, William Thomas? Nice to have a new hand on board."

"It's an honor to meet you, sir." William's voice quivered with excitement over meeting someone who spent his days digging the Cut.

"William can really play, Mr. Roberts," Hamilton informed him. "He almost knocked out the light bulb on that veranda."

Mr. Roberts put his arm around William's shoulder and gave it a squeeze. "Nice going! There's no sense in playing unless you're planning to be the best." Bud slapped his glove against the side of his leg and turned away. "Did your dad just hire on?" Mr. Roberts asked.

William nodded. "He's a new doctor at the hospital here."

"There's always need for a doc to bandage the little cuts and scrapes a fellow can get in the thick of battle. Count your blessings he's safe up topside. You been down yet?" Bud's father asked him.

William sighed and shook his head. "I'll probably leave Panama without ever getting into the Cut. This is already my second week."

"Oh, well, there's still plenty of time," the man said with a grin. "How about a trip with me one day into the hottest, noisiest place this side of you-know-where? The company down there isn't so good, if you know what I mean. But a spot on a steam shovel, free of charge, might make up for it."

"Hurray! When can we go?" William almost choked on his words.

"Just leave it to me," Mr. Roberts said. "Nothing is too good for a real slugger. So you boys played long enough?" Mr. Roberts asked, giving William's shoulder a final pat.

"Never!" Jeremy shouted.

"Let's hit a few then. William is up first," Mr. Roberts announced. While the other boys dashed to their places, Bud stomped to second base, then turned and glared angrily at William.

Mr. Roberts's first pitch drifted over the center of the plate and hung there, waiting to be hit. William gave it a hard smack. It sailed over the infield and headed straight for the same veranda he had hit earlier. Even through it fell short into a mud hole, the boys yelled their congratulations.

"You almost did it again," yelled Jeremy.

"You'd better be careful, or you'll have to buy those people some new screen," Carl shouted with admiration.

When Bud got up to bat, his dad's pitches flew toward the plate like comets, then sank down and inside at the worst moment for the batter.

"Your dad rubbed dynamite on that ball," Jeremy shouted.

"You can do it," Hamilton yelled.

But Bud struck out in three straight pitches. As the third ball hit the catcher's glove, Bud hurled the bat halfway to first base and stomped off. The other boys stared in silence.

"I'll deal with you when we get home," Mr. Roberts growled at his son. "I don't want to have to tell you ever again about showing your temper."

William couldn't believe the scene. It had been years since he had seen a kid throw a bat. No doubt about it, Bud Roberts had a very bad temper. But, William decided, Bud's father only seemed to make it worse.

CHAPTER

SIXTEEN

William's life began to take on a routine. He played baseball most mornings. Because of the increasing number of slides, spectators were no longer allowed near the stretch of the Cut at the village center. So he was always home by noon, eager to see the work on the stretch there and exchange barbs with Victoria when she was able to meet him.

William's one real problem was Bud. Even though William had tried hard to be friends, Bud seemed to keep track of every hit or throw either of them made, and as time went on, he grew more and more angry when William made a good play.

One morning the rain became so dense that the boys

couldn't see the pitcher's mound from home plate, so they piled onto the Robertses' large veranda. A baby toddled in and out of the room, pulling a toy lamb by a string. Two older children practiced handstands in the hall. Jeremy tossed the baseball into the air, just missing the ceiling.

"Let me see the ball a minute," Carl asked.

When Jeremy flipped the ball to him, Carl tossed it toward an empty basket that had once held a flower pot. It fell short, hitting the front of the basket and rolling back toward the boys. Hamilton scooped it up and gave it a toss.

"Good shot," Jeremy said as it fell in.

"I've got an idea." Hamilton reached out to retrieve the ball. "Everybody take turns trying to hit the basket. If you miss, you're out."

From their places on the floor, the boys each took a turn. Bud went first. He beamed as the ball went in. Then Jeremy threw and missed. Howard, Carl, and William made their first shots, but eventually only William and Bud were left.

By the time the two boys had each thrown several times without missing, Bud's face was red and his jaw set. William knew how he felt. This was a duel. Telling himself that the outcome didn't matter, William stretched his arms over his head and lobbed the ball. It floated in. Bud wiped his palms on his pants, aimed, and released a gentle toss. The ball hit the floor short of the basket. William had won.

"Wow!"

"Nice one!"

"Way to go!" the others shouted. Carl leaned over and gave William a congratulatory slap on the back.

"Nice one! Way to go!" Bud mimicked. He reached over and pounded William's back too hard, putting his bulk and strength into the blow.

"Ow!" William shouted and shot to his feet. "What are you doing?"

Bud jumped up and held up his clenched fists in front of him. "Can't you take a compliment?"

"Hey," Jeremy said, pushing his way between them. "Calm down. It was only a stupid game."

"I didn't mean anything," Bud vowed as he sank down again, his face burning. William hesitated, trying to decide whether or not to leave.

In the awkward silence, Hamilton fished the ball out of the basket and tossed it to Jeremy. "Try to hit this," he said. He stood and placed the basket on his head, holding it steady with one hand.

Before Jeremy had time to throw, Bud found his voice. "You look like one of those coloreds who carry all the stuff on their heads."

Hamilton began to prance around, the basket perched on his head. "Yes, sir," he mocked. He bent over in a deep bow, and a few dried leaves floated to the floor.

Everyone except William cackled. Bud laughed the loudest. Then he said, "My dad told us about a colored man in the Cut who used to fill his wheelbarrow, then have another fellow help him lift it onto his head so he could carry it to the fill train. Have you ever heard of anything so stupid?" The boys giggled.

"I saw some women carrying stacks of firewood on their heads," Howard said. "Can you believe that?"

William was relieved that everyone seemed to have forgotten the episode, but he didn't like these guys making fun of someone who could have been Victoria. "I know a girl from Jamaica who can carry a gigantic stack of books on her head and not drop one," William said.

"Working at your house?" Howard asked.

"She used to. Now she's just a friend."

Bud snickered. The others stared. "You can't be friends with a colored girl."

"I am, though," William said. "She even took me into the jungle to see a French excavator. She knows all about the jungle and French excavators and poison frogs and lots of other things."

"The jungle!" Carl said with amazement.

"You're lying," Bud challenged. "Your parents would never let you be friends with a colored girl, or go into the jungle either."

"Yes they would," William replied defensively.

"I don't believe you."

"Me neither," Hamilton echoed.

William bristled. "Then come to the Cut and meet her," he said as he put his hand on the door. "You'll see. Noon. At the edge of the field closest to my house."

CHAPTER

SEVENTEEN

William squished through the waterlogged grass. Inviting the boys to meet Victoria had been more absurd than the French plan to dig Culebra Cut down to sea level.

Steam and mist caused by the recent shower rose from the ground. Steam shovels and flatcars stood idle on the hill while the crews took their dinner break. Soon this whole field would be shaped into terraces in an attempt to prevent further slides.

When he reached the edge, Victoria was looking at a deep, jagged crevice. "Have you seen this new crack, Snowman? It's huge! The next slide is going to be even worse than the last one."

"I may have done something really stupid," William said, his voice quaking.

"You mean to say you dug this crack?" she teased.

"I'm serious," he said with a groan. "I invited the fellows I play ball with to meet you." Victoria's smile vanished. "I was sure they would like you. Besides, they thought I was lying about you being my friend." Sweat beaded on William's face. "But maybe I should have asked you before I asked them."

Victoria glared at him, then looked across the field. "You sure should have."

But it was too late to do anything about it. William's friends were chugging toward them like locomotives on the move.

"Maybe it will be all right," Victoria said as she pulled herself up to her full height and clasped her hands behind her back to keep them from shaking. "They are your friends, after all."

When the boys reached them, William made the introductions. "Victoria, this is Bud, Hamilton, Jeremy, Howard, and Carl." Victoria nodded. "Fellows, this is my friend Victoria."

"Hello," said Carl. "He was telling the truth, all right."

"Shut up, Carl," Bud said with a snarl. The other boys stared silently. Then Bud turned to William and continued. "I knew you'd be this kind, the way you waved at coloreds and didn't even know the difference between gold and silver. You've got a problem with your taste in friends."

"I thought *you* were my friend," William retorted.

Bud took a step forward. He was so close that William could count his freckles. "No friend of mine hangs around with coloreds."

"Let's get out of here," Jeremy said, pulling on Bud's arm. Bud shook him off.

Anger welled up in William. "You have the manners of a pig, Bud Roberts," he shouted. "Why don't you go practice your batting."

The next instant Bud's head smacked into William's stomach, knocking him onto his back. William rolled over and struggled to his feet, his clothes thick with mud. He was hardly back on his feet when Bud's fist landed in his middle. This time Bud sailed to the ground with him and planted himself on William's chest. William tried to twist out from under him, first to one side and then the other, but the boy was seated as firmly as a slide on the bottom of the Cut. Bud smashed his fist into William's nose and pounded his eye. William's face screamed with pain.

"Get off him, Roberts," Carl shouted.

"Yeah, let him up," Jeremy urged. "He's had enough."

"It's their fight," Hamilton countered. "What did he think he was doing, calling Bud a pig?"

William turned his head. Out of the corner of his

eye, he got a blurry look at Victoria backing across the
field toward a stand of young trees. William did not
blame her for leaving. The others, intent on the fight,
seemed not to notice.

Bud scooted back and pounded William's stomach
again. "This will teach you not to mix with coloreds."

No one saw Victoria gliding back toward the group.
Between two fingers she carried a large leaf folded into
a small pouch. In a single motion, she released the
end of the leaf and flicked its contents toward Bud's
back. Her aim was perfect.

"Bud," Hamilton yelled. "A gigantic bug just landed
on your back."

Bud shot up as though hit by lightning. "Where?
Where is it? Get it off," he yelled.

Hamilton pointed. "There. Climbing up your back
toward your neck. It looks like one of those giant ants,
about an inch long."

"Get it off me, you toad!"

"Let me find a stick," Hamilton said, searching
the ground.

"Get it off now!" Bud screamed as he shook the collar of his shirt. Sensing the motion, the ant halted.
Like a hot needle, its stinger plunged into Bud's back.

Bud shrieked, and the ant stabbed him a second
time. His face a deep red, Bud shrieked again. Finally
Jeremy pulled up a thick stalk of grass and brushed off
the ant, while Bud howled in pain.

Hamilton took Bud's arm and led him across the field toward home, flanked by Jeremy and Howard.

Carl hesitated. "You going to be all right?" he asked William.

"I guess so," William mumbled as he struggled to his feet. Carl looked at Victoria. Her face was so set it might have been carved of stone. "I wish I could have been more help," he said, then slowly followed the other boys across the field.

William balanced unsteadily on his feet. One eye was red and runny. His bleeding nose was already swollen, his lip cut.

"That boy got you pretty good, Snowman." William pulled out his handkerchief and dabbed at his bloody nose. Victoria slipped an arm under his elbow.

"I saw you leave," William muttered. "Why in the world did you come back?"

"To deliver the ant, of course."

William's head hurt too badly to turn toward her. "You put that ant on Bud?"

"Of course. How else do you think a tree ant got on his back?"

"Thanks," he said through his bulging lip. "You probably saved my life."

"You're welcome. And I probably did," Victoria said.

William took a wobbly step. "There goes my trip into the Cut," he moaned. "I'll never get down there now."

CHAPTER

EIGHTEEN

"You can't judge a book by its cover," his mother said to his father as they came out of the kitchen.

William's father positioned himself in the doorway to the veranda so that the breeze would hit his back. His mother perched on the edge of the wicker rocker and reached over to pat William's knee. It was evening, and his eye was black and swollen closed. His nose was the size of a small balloon. When he moved, he felt like he had been kicked in the stomach by a horse.

"We tried giving you more freedom, William, but it just didn't work," his father began. "The Cut is just too dangerous. There are more slides on this side all the time. Consequently you will not be allowed to go there unless I am along."

Knowing that his parents' reaction to his fight would be irrational didn't make their decision any easier to accept. "Bud Roberts does this to me," he grumbled through his expanding lip, "and you won't let me go to the Cut because of the slides? It doesn't make any sense."

"All right," Dr. Thomas said gravely. "We are also afraid that Bud will find you there and do this to you again. But each day the Cut becomes more dangerous, and it is our responsibility to protect you."

"As long as you keep to the main streets in the village, you'll be safe from the slides and that boy too," Mrs. Thomas added.

William was so angry that he wanted to cry. He shouted instead. "You're both crazy! I might as well not be in Panama." His outburst got him nothing except an evening alone in his room.

When Dr. Thomas was finally able to go with his son to the Cut at the end of that first week, Victoria was not there. William missed the Cut, but he missed Victoria even more. He knew he never should have invited the others to meet her without asking her first. Now she'd probably never want to see him again. Why hadn't he ever asked her where she lived? At least then he could go and apologize.

Every day he walked into the center of the village,

hoping she would be there. One morning, a week and a half after his fight with Bud, he had just stepped onto the boardwalk leading to the commissary when he saw her.

There was no mistaking the straight back and the yellow wrap on her head. She was rushing along on the opposite side of the road ahead of him. He wondered if she was hurrying because she had seen him. He wanted to call out to her but was sure she would run away if he did. Crossing the road, he made his way after her.

Past the headquarters building sprawled the public market, a large, covered pavilion where women and men from the countryside sold fruits, vegetables, and other wares. Victoria slipped through the wide entrance into the thick crowd. She stopped at a table, dickered with a woman, took a few pieces of fruit, then disappeared into the crowd again, her yellow head wrap like a signal flag.

Out of the market and back along the main street, William scurried after her. Not far from the YMCA, she rounded a building and disappeared.

William peeked around the corner and saw her moving swiftly along a dark, narrow street lined with decaying buildings. He followed her, hugging the shadows.

On balconies and porches, ropes sagged with laundry. A woman with strong, dark arms and a red head wrap was busy at one of the lines. If she noticed William, she did not let him know. A pack of children, dust coating their dark skin like flour, laughed as they chased one another among the huts. When he reached them, they fell silent, their staring eyes like bleached shells on wet sand.

The street ended, and Victoria followed a lightly worn path into the forest. William stopped. He had already strayed from the main streets of Culebra, and his parents would no doubt consider this the jungle. He swallowed hard as he stepped onto the path.

Huts and shacks made of everything from bamboo to packing crates dotted the undergrowth. Voices in many languages competed with noise from the Cut. Chickens ran free, pecking at the dark earth.

Suddenly the path narrowed and curved. The huts ended and trees closed in, blocking the sunlight. Bushes and vines fought to dominate the floor. William imagined thick snakes, poisonous frogs, and spiders bigger than his hand, but among the green he saw only brightly colored birds and flowers, ants, and a few beetles.

Careful to keep his distance, he followed Victoria along the serpentine trail. Once she paused, and William ducked behind a tree. When he came out again, she had disappeared. His heart pounded with the fear that he had lost her, but he kept walking. A moment later he saw a shack of cast-off wood and metal slumped in a yard once cleared but now swallowed by the undergrowth. Victoria hurried up the steps and disappeared inside.

Like the Thomases' house, this one stood on stilts, but it looked no larger than their living room. A tin tub and several white enamel basins were stacked in the corner of the tiny porch. A jumble of plants in wooden boxes and earthenware pots littered the railing and the floor.

As William drew nearer, he could hear someone moaning inside. Part of him wanted to turn and run back to the bright sunlight of Culebra's main road. But Victoria was his friend. Suddenly the moans exploded into coughing. Between the coughs William heard Victoria's voice.

Slowly he mounted the steps. The smell of rotting fruit and sickness drifted out to him from behind the gray cloth that served as a door. He turned his head aside for fresh air, gritted his teeth, and peered into the dimness. It was as though dusk lay in wait there, ready to spring upon the world. There was just enough light for William to see. And what he saw made his stomach churn.

CHAPTER

NINETEEN

On a cot in the corner lay a thin and wasted man. His wet clothes hung on him like rags on a scarecrow. His black hair and beard were matted and damp. With one dark hand, he grasped his chest.

Victoria stood at a crude table of split logs, her head bowed, her arms moving resolutely as she squeezed juice from the fruit she had bought. A chain of coughs erupted from the man, making her work faster. Kneeling beside the bed, she lifted the man's head and held a bowl of juice to his lips.

"Drink a little, Father. It will help."

Each time the man sipped, he sputtered and coughed, and she moved the bowl away, returning it to his lips when his coughing had eased. His head finally rolled toward her in sleep, and she rested it gently on the cot.

When Victoria rose she saw William standing in the doorway, not knowing what to say. Her face stiffened, but the tears that streaked her face kept coming. "Why are you here?" she asked.

William took a step forward and let the curtain close behind him. A whisper was all he could manage. "I wondered why you hadn't come back. I thought . . . I thought you were angry at me. I guess I know now why you stayed away," he finished lamely as he looked at the sick man.

"I guess you do."

William took a breath through his mouth. "I want to help. My father is a doctor. Let me get him."

"Doctors have helped enough already," she said bitterly.

"What's wrong with him?"

"The doctor said it's malaria."

"Malaria?" he repeated with surprise.

"He's been getting worse and worse even though he has been drinking quinine for a long time."

Victoria dipped a rag in water and wrung it out. Kneeling again, she carefully wiped her father's forehead, then returned to the table to squeeze more juice.

"All he used to talk about was the promise of a good life in the Canal Zone. 'Ten cents an hour for most any laboring job,' he would tell my mother. 'We can save enough money to buy a bit of land back home. And the children will have better schools.'" Her words flew like darts. "Well, I have never seen a schoolroom in Panama with fewer than a hundred black children in it. And I didn't see that for very long. Ruined dreams and sickness are all we ever got from this miserable ditch."

"But it's not the canal's fault," William said. "There's hardly any yellow fever left, and anyone with malaria is treated free of charge. People just get sick sometimes. It's bad luck."

"People work until they are too sick to do any more," Victoria argued, her voice shaking. "Then the bosses throw them away like the insides of these mountains."

"That's totally wrong. The canal's given thousands of people work, food, money, and decent places to live."

The muscles in Victoria's neck tensed. "There aren't any nice buildings with screens around them for us, Snowman. In fact there's hardly any place at all for us to live except run-down buildings in the cities or the bush. My father says living in Panama City or Colón is like living in a crowded ant hole. So we carved our own place out of the jungle."

The man in the bed moaned and coughed. His face twisted in pain. William half expected him to die that very second. Victoria made the man sip from the bowl of juice again. When he fell back to sleep, she stayed beside the bed, stroking his wet hair.

"Can't your mother get help?" William asked quietly.

"She's not here. She took the little ones with her to Cristobal, where she got a job in the laundry. She wanted us to go too, so she could continue to care for Father, but he wasn't that sick. He said he'd be better in no time and that I was big enough to look after him."

"Victoria, your father ought to be in the hospital at Culebra or maybe even in Ancon," William said more boldly. He met her glare head on. "Look," he said finally. "The doctor your father saw must have made a mistake. Malaria doesn't have a cough with it."

"You know that for a fact?" she asked.

"I know that for a fact."

Victoria wiped her eyes on her sleeve. "A man who came from our village in Jamaica said the same thing. He said it was not malaria at all, but a duppy."

"I didn't mean a duppy," William said anxiously. "I meant a different disease."

Victoria shook her head, tossing his idea aside. "An explosion in the Cut killed a man who was standing right next to Father. There wasn't enough of him left to bury properly." William shuddered. "The man from my village swears the dead man's duppy is causing this sickness."

William motioned toward the strings of cowrie

shells hanging on the wall. "Wouldn't those drive a duppy away?"

Victoria rose and returned the bowl to the table. "Not once the duppy's in the house. Then it takes more than shells to get rid of it. Only a healer can make the duppy leave my father alone."

"A healer! What's that?"

"A person who heals, of course. And with him this bad, it's no use going to just any healer," she said. "It's got to be a powerful one. It will have to be Mother James."

"The hospital, Victoria. He needs to be in the hospital," William said stubbornly.

"Mother James doesn't like children," she continued, ignoring William's comment. "I heard she once turned a disrespectful girl into a frog. But I can't find a grown-up to go for me. There are duppies around her place, and most everyone is too afraid to go near it. I'll have to go myself."

William bit his lip and turned toward the door. Lines of light slid through the gaps at the sides of the curtain. He knew he ought to convince her to get her father to the hospital or else go straight to his own father. But she was the best friend he had in Panama—she had saved him during the fight and taken him into the jungle. Besides, she knew about lots of things he had never heard of. Maybe she knew about a different kind of healing.

Like the motes of dust floating in the light, his decision became clear. He turned back into the dimness. "I'll go with you."

Victoria's head jerked up when he said it. "You'll go? You'll go with me to see Mother James?"

"I'm not sure it will work. But you're my friend, so I'll go with you."

"It might be dangerous."

William almost smiled. "I'm not really afraid of duppies or of being turned into a frog. I'm only worried that we will be wasting time when your father needs help right away."

"We won't be wasting time," Victoria insisted.

"There's one condition though. If it doesn't work, we will get him to the hospital."

"It will work," she assured him.

"If it doesn't, we take him to the hospital," he repeated. Victoria raised her eyebrows but said nothing. "So where is the healer?" William continued. "And when do we go? It'll have to be sometime when I can sneak out."

"We'll go tonight at midnight. Meet me at the head of the street." Victoria smiled.

"All right."

"Thanks, Snowman. You're a real friend."

"You're welcome," he said. "Before I go, why don't we take those boards off the windows? Fresh air might help his cough."

"They help keep other duppies out," she said patiently.

He nodded and backed out the door, knowing that if his parents found out his plan, they would lock him up for the rest of his life.

CHAPTER

TWENTY

The midnight fog coiled around William's ankles like hungry snakes. Just as he was telling himself that he was not frightened, something scampered over his foot. He jerked it away and tried to erase a vision of what it might have been. No, he wasn't afraid of a healer. The things that frightened him were real! Wiping moisture from his face, he swallowed his fear and prayed that Victoria's father would live through the night.

When William came to the corner where he and Victoria were to meet, he saw her, cloaked in fog and darkness. Her eyes glowed beneath the brim of a hat pulled low.

"How is your father?"

"The same," she said quietly. "Are you sure you want to go?"

"Yes," he answered.

Victoria handed him a string tied with shells and bones. "This is not strong enough to work against the healer. She's too powerful. But it will shield you from duppies." William took the string skeptically. "Don't look directly into her eyes," Victoria continued. "Her look can seize you." Victoria held up a small piece of charcoal. "I'm going to make you colored."

"Don't you think that's overdoing it?"

"Not one bit," she said. "Mother James doesn't like white folks at her healings. No telling what she would do if she found out. And don't worry, it washes off. You're not going to stay that way forever."

"If she's got powerful eyes, a little charcoal isn't going to fool her."

"Her eyes have power all right, but she doesn't see very well. And there won't be much light. As long as you keep your mouth shut and your head down, she won't know." As Victoria spread charcoal over his face and up the sides of his nose, her fingers shook.

"Watch out for the nose," he said.

"Still hurts, huh?" she asked as she gently dabbed his nose with black.

"I doubt that it will ever be the same."

"Just a little more. You do your hands," she said,

handing him the charcoal. Finally she smiled at their handiwork. "Keep your hair under your hat, and you'll be a respectable Jamaican boy." As she turned and led the way along the street, William pulled his hat over his eyes and tucked his bangs inside it.

At the end of the street, they passed between two buildings and into the forest. Victoria seemed to know where she was going. After a few moments, she stopped in front of a bamboo hut roofed with thatch. Through the gaps between the poles, faint light glowed. William could make out strings of teeth, feathers, and bones hung around the doorway.

A low voice drifted out to them, rising and falling in a quiet chant. Timidly Victoria stepped over to a tree and rang the bell hung there. The chants stopped, and a woman pulled back the curtain in the doorway.

Suddenly William's legs turned to rubber, and he understood why Victoria was afraid. The old woman was more frightening than anyone he had ever seen. A dark face, sharp and angular like the head of an ax, topped her long, thin frame. High cheekbones emphasized her large mouth. Wild gray hair spread in an orb around her head, making her look even taller than she was.

But it was her eyes that drew William in. Narrowly set, they were large and protruding, as though made to see more than most people dare.

"Young ones!" she thundered.

CHAPTER

TWENTY-ONE

The healer took Victoria by the shoulders and spun her around and around, all the while muttering words that William could not understand. "Pass in," she said, each word ringing with power. She did the same with William, then followed him in.

William sat on the straw mat where Victoria was already settled, her legs folded and her large shoes tucked under her skirt. Awkwardly William imitated her position.

Careful to avoid the eyes of the healer, he looked around the hut. Dried herbs, feathers, shells, teeth, and bones were tied to the walls in long rows. Gourds filled with dried plants, dirt, and seeds lined the floor.

Smells from fertile soil and pungent plants quarreled in the air.

"Why have grown-ups sent children to do their business?" the healer's voice boomed.

"Nobody sent us, ma'am," Victoria said, her voice quivering. "You see, my father is very sick and there was no one else to come."

"This is your brother?" William felt the old woman's gaze bore into him.

"My cousin, ma'am. He was born not able to speak."

"Tell me about your father's illness, child," Mother James said.

"He's been coughing and hurting in his chest, and so feverish that from one minute to the next he looks like he might not last. A doctor at Culebra said it's malaria, but the medicine does no good." Victoria's account reminded William of the way his father's patients talked about their symptoms, except that Victoria chose her words more carefully.

"How long has the illness been with him?" the healer asked.

"It started two months back. There was an explosion," Victoria explained. "A man working with my father went to scoop up some broken rock, and his shovel hit the charge on some dynamite. The blast sent him flying straight toward heaven. Father was thrown up against the side of a rock and was unconscious for a while, but afterward he seemed to be all right. He kept saying he was lucky to be alive, since he was the one who had been breaking up the rock. After that he gradually got sicker until now he is barely alive. Nothing seems to help."

William glanced sideways at his friend's face. Her eyes were focused on the mat in front of her.

"Did they bury the man properly?" Mother James asked.

Victoria shook her head, her eyes still lowered. "No, ma'am. They couldn't. There was no way to nail the man's cuffs to the coffin so that his spirit couldn't wander off."

"Then sure as the sun rises, the man's duppy is seeking revenge on your father. He's making mischief on the one he thinks should have been taken in his place. By now he's moved right into your home."

William felt compelled to glance up. He saw the old woman move from one group of herbs to the next, touching the sprigs and bundles tied to the bamboo. When she turned, William looked down hastily, hoping she would not notice.

"I need to drive him away," Victoria said, her voice hushed with sadness. "Can you help me?"

Mother James walked over to a log table and picked up a gourd. With fingers like stiff, knotted rope, she pinched off bits of dry leaves, twigs, and seeds and dropped them inside. She placed the gourd on the table and pulled two strings from a tangled pile.

Again William watched as she circled the hut, her eyes intent upon the things on the walls. She removed four shells and tied two onto each string, then divided a group of feathers between them. A few bones and a sprig from a dried plant were added.

Suddenly the old woman whirled around. Her white hair swayed like the seeds of a milkweed plant ready to fly into the wind. Before William could look away, her eyes met his. Her eyes pulsed like flames, capturing him, and he struggled to look away. He tried to move his hand toward Victoria, but it clung to his knee as though glued there. His voice stayed silent while his mind screamed for help. Gradually the light in the hut dimmed, and everything went blank.

The next thing he knew, Victoria was helping him sit up. His head ached, and his stomach felt queasy. He could hear himself panting. "You're all right now," Victoria said nervously. "You fainted."

He bit his lip to keep from speaking. Worried that the sweat sliding down his face would streak the charcoal, he pulled his hat further down over his eyes.

Mother James seated herself on the mat facing them, and William stared at her twisted hands. One clutched the gourd filled with herbs and seeds, and the other the two strings and a rope.

"There are some things you must do," she said. The woman held out the gourd. "You must mix these herbs with water and sprinkle them over your father. It will get the duppy off his chest and keep him off." Victoria reached out to take the gourd, but the healer was not ready to give it up. The woman picked some large flat seeds out of it. "You must also fix five of these seeds above your door with mud. They will keep the duppy from entering your house again."

Victoria nodded and put out a trembling hand. Mother James dropped the seeds one after the other into the girl's hand. Where each seed landed, a welt formed on her skin. Victoria clenched her teeth and closed her palm tightly around them.

"There is one ingredient still needed. And it is you who must get it." Victoria held her breath. "The mud you use to fix the seeds above the door must come from the bottom of the Cut."

"From the bottom of the Cut?" Victoria gasped.

"Yes. The duppy is afraid of anything from the Cut." The old woman's voice rose impatiently. "Without the soil the duppy will continue to invade your house and bother your father until he dies."

"But there's no way to get into the Cut without being seen. People work there day and night," Victoria protested.

On the mat the healer laid the two strings she had made. "Wear these. They will make you invisible to the eyes of white men."

William looked at Victoria out of the corner of his eye. She looked as if she might cry.

Finally the old woman laid a slender rope and a handful of small shells and feathers on the mat. Swiftly her aged fingers slipped a row of loose knots into the rope, then slid a feather, a shell, a twig, or a bone into each knot before pulling it tight.

"For your cousin." William jumped. Even by pressing on his knees, he couldn't keep his legs from shaking. "He should hang it near the door of the white boy who torments him, and he will not have to worry about that boy again."

How could this old woman know someone was bothering me? William thought frantically. He didn't dare look up, and he didn't dare take the rope.

Victoria gathered up the rope, strings, and gourd. "We'll do as you say, Mother James," she whispered.

CHAPTER

TWENTY-TWO

A light breeze had chased away the fog, leaving the night air fresh and cool. But sweat glued William's shirt to his body, and he did not notice the change. Without speaking he and Victoria wove their way among the shacks.

"Why didn't you tell me it would be like that?" William whispered when at last they reached the end of the path and stepped onto the narrow street.

Victoria stared at him. "I did tell you!"

"How did her eyes get hold of me like that?"

"I warned you that she would put a spell on you if you looked at her. It was no wonder she did. You didn't even have enough respect to look away."

William recalled the eerie eyes that had bound him like cords. "That was scary," he said, his shaking fingers fanning his shirt back and forth against his chest.

Quietly they made their way down the street. Here and there a light burned in a window. A baby's cry echoed between the buildings, and hushed notes of a father's song floated out to them. Gradually the vision of the healer's eyes faded in William's mind.

William took a deep breath. "The smell and close air probably made me faint. Or it was some sort of trick."

"Then how did she know about that boy?"

William was silent as he thought it over. "Maybe she noticed my nose. It's still swollen."

"She can't see that well," Victoria retorted. Just then the ground shook from an explosion in the Cut. "Well I haven't got time to talk about it. I've got to find some way to get into that ditch."

"I thought she was going to give you some kind of medicine. Sticking those seeds above your door with mud from the Cut can't possibly cure your father!"

"You're the one who was captured by her eyes. You should know that what she says is true."

William pushed back his hat. The white skin between the line of charcoal and his hat band reflected the moonlight. He felt confused.

"All right, all right. For a moment maybe it seemed as if she had some kind of power over me. But no matter what, mud from the Cut isn't going to help him. Besides, this part of the Cut is off-limits to everyone except the workers."

"You think you know everything about everything, Snowman." Victoria's eyes sliced through the darkness as she picked up the pace.

William stopped and watched her walk away, amazed that she was actually going to try to go down there. But he was unwilling to abandon his friend. "I'm going too," he said.

Victoria turned. "Even though you don't think the soil will help?"

"Sure," he said seriously. Then he grinned. "I've always wanted to go into the Cut, and it doesn't look like I'll get there any other way. Besides, it's too dangerous for one person to go down there alone."

She peered out from under the brim of her hat. "You're saying that it will be less dangerous if you go too? You can't even walk into the jungle without getting stuck in the mud."

William hoped that the charcoal and darkness hid his crimson face. "So what? I can help if you get into trouble. Besides, I know a great way into the Cut. At least I think I do. There used to be a place behind the YMCA that was almost like a ramp."

Victoria handed William one of the strings from the healer and put the other over her head.

"You think this is going to make us invisible?" William asked.

"Mother James said 'invisible to white men.'"

"I'm white, and I can see you."

"You don't look very white to me."

William touched his skin and laughed. He passed the string over his head and fell in beside her, the shells, bones, and feathers bouncing on his chest. Hundreds of times William had imagined going into the Cut, but never in the dark. He clenched his teeth to keep them from chattering.

When they reached the main road, they searched for signs of the canal police. Lights for crews planting dynamite dotted the chasm. To their left, the ladders were lit like a constellation.

As they crossed the road and approached the edge, William searched for the place where the mountaintop had slid into the Cut. The soles of his boots stuck in the dark, slick clay. Suddenly the vegetation beneath his feet disappeared, and his dim shape lunged forward and vanished.

"Snowman?" Victoria whispered, afraid that he had slipped over the edge.

William scrambled to his feet and backed away. "There's a huge crack here. I almost fell into it." A three-foot-wide crevice between the field and the Cut swallowed the moonlight.

"This is like the one in the field behind your house," Victoria whispered.

"Except wider! This cliff is ready to drop! How

about taking some of the soil right here?"

Victoria shook her head. "Very soon it will be at the bottom of the Cut, but not quite soon enough."

They jumped the crack and looked down. "There's a slope," William said excitedly. "I don't know if this is the same one, but it looks just as good. There's even a steam shovel like last time." The top of a giant machine glittered in the darkness.

"Once in a while those slides do some good. It shouldn't be too hard to get down there," Victoria said as she coiled the rope inside the gourd and set the gourd under her hat. "This ground is as runny as Jamaican molasses. We'd better get down there and back before this cliff comes sliding down on us."

William stepped down the clay slope. Immediately his feet slipped out from under him. He threw both hands behind him to stop himself. "Ugh," he said, standing and flicking the mud off his hands.

"Go down sideways," Victoria instructed, her feet parallel to the rim, her oversized shoes balancing on top of the clay like snowshoes on a drift. William followed. Here and there large rocks emerged, giving them traction.

As they rounded a large boulder, they got a better look at the steam shovel ahead of them. Mud and rock covered all but the top third of it. Just downhill from the machine, a section of track stuck out of the ground straight as a flagpole.

Maybe Victoria was right, William thought. Maybe nature was as set against the canal now as it had been when the French had tried to build it. But tomorrow the workers would start again. They would bring in picks, shovels, and another steam shovel to dig out this one. And if another slide occurred, they would dig that one out too, and again and again and again until the canal was finished.

Suddenly the earth trembled, and the roar of an explosion thundered toward them. Across the Cut, tons of rock and dirt flew from the side of the cliff.

CHAPTER

TWENTY-THREE

William slid toward Victoria, who was crouched with her head on her knees. "Are you all right?" he called. She nodded and stood up. Even in the darkness, he could see her shaking. "That blast was close."

"I'm going on," Victoria said.

In silence they slid and scrambled down, then slogged through the mire across a set of rails to another steam shovel, this one in working condition. The floor of the shovel stood a foot above their heads. High on its side gleamed the marking, "U.S.◆212."

"Just think, this could be the steam shovel Teddy Roosevelt sat in! You've seen that famous photograph, haven't you?

"Who's Teddy Roosevelt?" Victoria asked.

William hesitated. Then he figured that there was little reason for a Jamaican to know much about the United States. "He was the president of the U.S. until two years ago. The one who got the canal going. He promised he would 'make the dirt fly,' and he did."

"'Make the mud slide' is more like it," Victoria countered. Suddenly she ducked behind the giant shovel, pulling William down beside her. "Look!" A headlight danced along the tracks to their left, then stopped.

"Maybe they're checking to see how much dirt and rock the explosion knocked loose," William whispered.

While Victoria and William hid beside the steam shovel, two lanterns descended from the engine and wove across the floor to the far wall, paused, then returned to the locomotive. Voices jockeyed through the air. The locomotive started up again and continued to trudge toward them, its huge light sweeping away the darkness like a broom attacking dust. Not far away it stopped again. The steam shovel where Victoria and William hid was frozen in the edge of its light.

"We're going to get caught!" William said.

"We've got to hide inside."

Silently Victoria and William stole to the side of the machine, sprang onto the ledge and into its open side. Two men carrying lanterns crossed the arc of light and walked straight toward the giant shovel, their legs and feet illuminated, their faces lost in darkness.

Victoria tucked her hat and the gourd under her and flattened herself close to the tall, iron seat. Squinting at the light that played on the boiler behind him, William tugged his hat down and rested his forehead on his bent knees.

Boots squashed through the mud and paused in front of the steam shovel. "This machine looks tilted."

The blood roared in William's ears. One lantern made its way around the side of the machine. Then suddenly it was thrust through the opening, and dull light spilled into the cab. A thin, white hand dangled the lantern above Victoria's shoes.

William held his breath and squeezed his lids closed. First the man would see Victoria glued to the floor and collar her. Then he would look farther back and find William. They would be hauled out of the Cut like criminals, and William's parents would stuff him in a book crate and ship him back to the United States.

The man swung the light toward the seat where Victoria was hiding and held it there. Then he turned and walked back to the other man. "A ground heave must have lifted one side," he muttered.

"Looks like it," the second man agreed. "Why are they blasting here anyway? The top of that cliff will be down here by the end of the week."

"Can't leave the engineers with nothing to do tomorrow," the first man said with a chuckle. "Let's check those charges."

Slowly William opened his eyes and Victoria raised her head. They watched silently as the lanterns sashayed along the base of the ramp they had descended. Finally the lights returned to the locomotive, and the engine continued slowly along the track.

Victoria clasped the necklace from the healer. "These spells are more powerful than Mother James told us. The slope we came down must have been spattered with dynamite and charges."

"And they're going to set them off any minute," said William nervously.

"We should be safe in here," Victoria said as she sat up. "They wouldn't risk blowing up a steam shovel."

"It's probably just a tiny blast anyway," William said more confidently. "Anything bigger might be dangerous, with that giant crack up there."

Victoria scooted to the side of the steam shovel.

"Where are you going?"

She stuffed her hat onto her head. "To get the mud." Holding the gourd in front of her, she lay down on her stomach and lowered herself from the cab. William could hear her scraping at the soil. A moment later she slipped back in, her hat pulled tight around her ears.

William slid back and positioned himself against the boiler. "We'd better get something between us and the explosion."

Victoria nodded and dropped down next to him.

For a while they sat silently, the sounds of the night far above them. William could feel Victoria shaking beside him. He knew he was shaking too. "This wasn't the way I'd pictured my first time on a steam shovel."

"It's a good thing your president didn't have to crawl around like this. His nice suit wouldn't have stayed white very long."

"How'd you know he was wearing a white suit?" William saw the edge of her grin in the moonlight. "You were pulling my leg again. You know who Teddy Roosevelt is! You've even seen the picture!"

Just then the air cracked. Dirt and rock pounded the steam shovel, flying through the openings and vibrating the sides like a drum. William and Victoria ducked their heads. Earth came down around them like rain. Then, like a summer downpour, it was over, and the air was still.

"Come on," Victoria said, "let's get out of here."

"Wait," William said. "Listen. Moaning—Do you hear it?"

Victoria nodded.

The sound bounced between the walls of the Cut, twisted, rose, swooped, and swelled. William and Victoria looked out. The wall they had descended earlier quivered in the moonlight.

William grabbed Victoria's arm. "It's the side of the Cut," he cried. "It's coming down! The blast must have knocked it loose!"

Suddenly the moan was smothered by a boom as the wall broke away and tons of mud and rock roared down into the Cut. The ground beneath them rose and tilted. In an instant the force of the slide lifted the steam shovel and tipped it onto its side. Victoria and William tumbled across the floor, screaming. As the shovel was carried to the middle of the Cut, mud and rock pushed their way inside. The door to the boiler flew open. Coal spilled out and mixed with the spoil.

Legs and arms churning against the rising fill, William caught hold of the boiler door and hung on. Victoria battled forward to grab the iron seat and braced her feet against it. At last the slide ground to a halt, depositing the steam shovel like a piece of trash, half buried.

"You hurt?" Victoria whispered as she pulled herself onto the bar that held the seat and looked around.

"My legs are stuck!" William cried as he threw aside handfuls of dirt and rock.

Victoria crawled toward him and dug frantically. "We'll get you out."

A whistle blew. Then others joined it, sounding the alarm. "Rescue crews will be everywhere in no time," William said.

"And maybe duppies too," Victoria said.

"I think I can get one leg out," William said. He held the edge of the steam shovel's tilted floor to steady himself and worked the leg back and forth, struggling against the weight and suction of the mud. Finally the leg came free. William bent over and helped Victoria dig out his other leg.

Weak and shaky, he followed her through the mud and rock to the front of the steam shovel, then inched along the shovel's prone crane. The ground was littered with boulders that moments before had been inside the mountain. "That slide could have killed us. If I hadn't been able to get hold of the door, I'd have been completely buried," William said as he crawled onto a huge rock.

Creeping and crawling from one dark boulder to the next, they picked their way across the floor. Where the rubble began to form a slope toward the rim, rails and ties were heaped together like pick-up sticks.

Halfway up the slope, Victoria stepped up the pace. Behind them crews with lanterns and electric lights were spreading out to survey the damage. Weighed down by his wet, muddy clothes, William struggled to keep up. He was sure Victoria was thinking about her father. When they rounded the top, William could hardly believe the amount of earth that had fallen away. The veranda of the YMCA was only yards from the edge of the Cut. Another large slide would send it over the side.

"I've got to get back," Victoria said as people and wagons rushed along the road to the place where the ladders had been. She reached a muddy hand under her hat and brought out the gourd. "I almost forgot," she said as she took out the rope. "Mother James said to hang it near that boy's door."

"All right. I've done so many crazy things tonight, one more is not going to make much difference." She was about to turn and bolt across the field, so he blurted, "I—I hope the potion makes your father better. Truly I do."

"It will. You'll see." Victoria stuffed the gourd under her hat and reached out to squeeze his muddy hand in her own. "Thank you, Snowman. For all your help."

"You're welcome," he said, but Victoria was already gone.

CHAPTER

TWENTY-FOUR

None of the people rushing toward the Cut seemed to notice the mud-caked boy trudging down the road. William looked for his father but did not see him. He took that as a good sign. Maybe no one had been hurt.

As he walked William fingered the shells and bones tied into the rope. It might be silly to hang it. It might be silly not to. He felt too mixed up to know.

William left the road and crept up to the cottage where Bud lived. Cupping his hands against the screen, he could see the basket the boys had used for the tossing game standing among the plants. With his fingertips, he worked Mother James's gift between the door frame and the screen. He stepped backed. At least in the darkness, none of it was visible.

As he walked along the main road again, fatigue and fear washed over him. He hoped the herbs and seeds Mother James had given Victoria would work. When he thought of the way the old woman's eyes had held him and how the man with the lantern had overlooked them in the steam shovel, he thought there might be a chance that they would make a difference. But what if they didn't? Sprinkling someone with an herb potion and sticking seeds above the door sounded useless.

So far he had gone along with Victoria. But what if her father died because of it? How was he supposed to decide? He had no idea what to do.

He turned onto the boardwalk approaching his house. Lights burned in every room. His father must have been called out. His mother would have looked into his room by now and discovered him gone. It didn't matter. That he would be in trouble was the least of his worries.

"Mother," he called as he crossed the veranda.

His mother rushed to the door and stared at the tired, filthy child in the doorway. "William! Are you hurt?"

"I'm fine."

Dr. Thomas dashed in from the dining room. "Your mother and I were crazy with worry! Where have you been?"

"You're home!" William said with relief. "I know I

will be punished, but I've got to have your help. Victoria's father is very sick. I sneaked out tonight to help, but what we did may not be enough. Please help him, Father."

"If her father is ill, he should go to the hospital," Dr. Thomas said in his calmest doctor's voice.

"He can't—and won't," William explained. "He's so ill, he's hardly alive. And Victoria won't go, because she's sure it won't help. You see, he went before, and a doctor diagnosed him with malaria. But coughing and chest pain don't go with malaria, do they?"

"No," his father agreed. "Might be pneumonia. With all this wetness and poor diets, it's pretty common. Do you know where he lives?"

"Yes. In the jungle, off a street near the YMCA."

"There's been a slide in the Cut, William. I'll have to find out if they can spare me for a while," Dr. Thomas said, turning toward the telephone.

William slid to the floor of the veranda and leaned his back against one of the wooden supports. "Tell Father to hurry, will you please?" he asked his mother.

In a few seconds his mother returned and handed him a piece of bread. "William, even though you may feel you are to blame if something terrible happens to Victoria's father, that's simply not true. Grown-ups are supposed to take care of children, not the other way around."

He sank his teeth into the crusty bread, and a tear

slid down his cheek. He wished Victoria could be eating some at that moment.

"It sounds unbelievable, but they haven't found anybody hurt yet," William's father announced as he returned. "We best be on our way." William smiled tiredly.

"Jonathan, do you really think William should go?" Mrs. Thomas asked. "It might be dangerous. And he's exhausted."

William pushed back his shoulders. "I'm not the least bit tired, and it's not dangerous. Besides, Father could never find it without me." As he struggled to his feet, he hoped the price of bringing his father with him would not be Victoria's friendship.

CHAPTER

TWENTY-FIVE

As they made their way through the forest, William finished telling his father about the healer and the trip into the Cut. Pink light coated the sky, but the shack where Victoria lived was draped in shadows. Above the door, embedded in globs of mud, were the five large, flat seeds.

William stepped onto the porch, and his father followed. William drew back the curtain and peered inside. Victoria sat next to her father's cot, asleep with her head in her hands.

"Let me speak with her first," William whispered to his father, who nodded. The boy closed his nose against the staleness, removed his hat, and stepped in, letting the curtain fall closed behind him.

"Victoria," he said as he moved toward the cot.

Victoria raised her head. "He's better," she said, her voice limp with fatigue. The man's wheeze was certainly less terrifying than the rattle of the day before, but his face was still damp and gray.

"I put up the seeds first thing, then sprinkled him with some of the herbs. And it's already working."

"I brought my father," William said quietly.

Victoria sprang to her feet. "This is my business! It's for me to take care of. And I was sure I could trust you!"

"My father knows healing too. He may be able to help." Victoria looked through him as though he were invisible.

William opened the curtain, his eyes begging her forgiveness, and his father stepped inside. "How do you do," Dr. Thomas said. "I have come to see about your father."

"How do you do," Victoria said stiffly. As he moved toward the bed, Victoria placed herself squarely between him and the bed. Dr. Thomas looked over her shoulder and studied the frail, wheezing man. "Your father needs to be in the hospital," he said gently.

"Mother James's cure is already making him better," Victoria said.

"William told me about the herbs," Dr. Thomas said. "Our medicine should be able to help even more."

"A doctor at the hospital has already helped," she said, her voice polite but determined. "He said it was malaria and gave him some horrible medicine that did no good at all."

"That doctor made a mistake. I can probably tell what is wrong with him if you will only let me look."

Victoria shook her head. "It doesn't matter now. Mother James's potion is helping him."

William stepped toward Victoria, searching for the words to convince her. Clumps of dried mud fell off his boots. "Wouldn't it be better if *two* kinds of healing worked to save your father?" he asked finally. Victoria stared at the floor, thinking. "Even if the herbs have helped," William continued, "wouldn't it be better to add another medicine?"

A moment later Victoria stepped away from the cot. "Your father may look. Maybe he is a better healer than that other doctor."

"I need some light. And fresh air would help too," Dr. Thomas said as he knelt beside the cot.

"Can we uncover the windows?" William asked. "A duppy can't get in now that the seeds are up, can it?"

"No, it can't," Victoria said.

"Duppy? What does that mean?" Dr. Thomas asked.

William hesitated. "It means that we can uncover the windows."

Together Victoria and William pulled off the boards. The light and air swept in like a smile.

Dr. Thomas took a stethoscope from his bag. Touching the man's chest made him curl with pain. "It's pneumonia, all right, but his fever has broken. His chest is noisy, but it's not as bad as it could be. It looks like he is past the crisis."

"I told you that," Victoria said.

Dr. Thomas turned to Victoria. "He's still very sick, though. We need to get him to the hospital. I promise that we will give him excellent care." Victoria looked at her father, thin and weak.

"They will feed him as much as he can hold," William added. "That's got to help him as much as anything else."

"Sometimes you are right, Snowman. And you are right about that." Quickly Victoria gathered the talismans from the wall, placed them in her hat, and lay the hat next to her father. Then she headed outside to collect the seeds from above the door.

"William," his father said. "I'd rather not leave this man just now. Do you have the strength to fetch a cart and driver from the hospital?"

"I'm on my way," William said with a quick nod. Before Dr. Thomas had time to put away his stethoscope, William was urging his weary legs along the path.

CHAPTER

TWENTY-SIX

Mrs. Thomas held out the spine of a book. "It's mold. Not so green that anyone would notice. But just give it time."

"It really happened!" William said as he slid a book from the shelf and turned it over in his hands. He couldn't wait to tell Victoria.

"You thought it might?" his mother asked.

"Victoria said so the day she unpacked the books. I thought she was just teasing me."

"I'll have to ship the books home," Mrs. Thomas declared. "This blasted humidity is as bad as snow." Just then the telephone rang, and she went into the hall to answer it. Soon she reappeared in the doorway.

"I'm not sure I should tell you this," his mother said, "but your father just telephoned from the hospital. They need to empty some of the beds, so they're sending Victoria's father to the hospital in Ancon on the next train. Of course Victoria's going with him. The train leaves in half an hour."

"I've got to go!" William said, dropping the book on the table and rushing into the hall for his hat. It hadn't occurred to him that they might be sent away without warning!

"Be careful! It's pouring out there," his mother cautioned.

"That doesn't matter," he called as he charged out the door.

As he raced along the road, he could see how much of the field behind the houses had fallen away. Most of the rest of it had turned to mud as steam shovels worked feverishly to carve terraces in the bank. Near the center of the village, a crowd had gathered to watch as workers pulled screens and timbers from the back veranda of the YMCA before the next slide could send it tumbling over the edge.

An umbrella broke away from the spectators and headed toward William. "Hey," Carl called with a grin. "Did you hear that Bud is leaving?" William stopped short and looked at Carl in amazement. "It's true. His father's been offered some high-paying job in the U.S. They're pulling out right away."

"No kidding!" William exclaimed.   "The spell worked!"

"What?" Carl asked.

"I'll tell you about it sometime," William said.   "But I've got to go right now."

"Say, how about coming over tomorrow?" Carl asked.

"Great! Maybe we can come back here and watch these guys take this place apart," William shouted as he loped along the road again. "I'll stop by."

Beyond the market a train idled at the station. Several ambulances stood next to it, rain bouncing off their roofs. Victoria waited beside one of them.

"Victoria," William shouted as he ran toward her. She raised her hand and waved. "My father telephoned," he said breathlessly when he reached her. "I'm really sorry you're going."

"I thought it might happen this way."

He could tell from her voice that she did not blame him. "Will you go to Cristobal to be with your mother?"

"Not until Father is better," she said. "I'll stay in Panama City with my great-aunt and uncle. They came to build the French canal but stayed on afterward. They have asked several times for us to come."

William wiped his hand over his wet face and stared at his feet. Water poured over the toes of his boots like miniature waterfalls. He had so many things to say, he didn't know where to begin. "You were right about the mold. The books are turning green, just the way you said. I thought you made it up."

"Why did you think that?" she asked.

"Because you always seem to be teasing me."

"You are easy to tease, Snowman. Say," she added as casually as she could, "did you hear about the new plan to deal with the slides in the Cut?"

William's eyes widened. "A new plan? I haven't heard about a new plan."

Two attendants pulled a stretcher out of the ambulance. One looked at Victoria and William and frowned. "This your father, pickney?" Victoria shook her head. The stretcher disappeared inside the train, and a few seconds later, the men stepped into the ambulance again.

"Well, are you going to tell me or not?" William asked.

"It's hard to believe they're going to do it," Victoria said, drawing out the story.

"What is it? What's the plan?" William said impatiently. The attendants carried another stretcher onto the train.

"That's him," Victoria said as the men came out of the ambulance with a third patient. When her father was safely aboard, she and William splashed through the water to the nearest passenger car.

"So?" William asked.

Victoria turned and grinned at William. "They're going to fill in the Cut and dig the canal somewhere else."

William hesitated for a split second. "You're doing it again. You have no mercy at all," he said, pretending to be angry. "This canal will be dug, no matter what. Just wait and see."

"They'll never get the best of these slides," Victoria protested.

The ambulance attendants stepped off the train and drove away. William knew he didn't have much time and didn't want to waste it arguing about the Cut. "You've been a great friend, Victoria. Thanks to you, I've seen a lot more of Panama than just steam shovels and dynamite. I'll really miss you."

Victoria looked down. "I'll miss you too, Snowman."

William reached into his pocket and pulled out the necklace Mother James had given him. "Just in case you run into any duppies or need to become invisible," he said, holding it out to Victoria.

"You may need it. I've got these." She opened her hand and showed him the five seeds Mother James had given her, still caked with mud from the Cut.

"And I still have this one," William said, reaching inside his shirt and showing her one of the strings of cowrie shells she had given him. Victoria grinned and took the necklace.

A railway attendant walked along the line of railway

cars, slamming the doors. Victoria hurried up the steps and turned in the doorway.

"I'll write if you send me your great-aunt and uncle's address," William said. "Maybe I can even visit sometime too. My parents are bound to take me to Panama City some day."

"All right," she called as the attendant reached up and slammed the door.

The locomotive was gathering steam when William remembered. "Bud's leaving Panama! He's going right away!" he shouted through the door. Victoria shook her head and waved to show that she had not heard him. As William waved back, he vowed to write her about Bud as soon as he got her new address. Then he stepped away to escape the hot spray.

More about the Panama Canal

The dream of building a canal across the isthmus of Panama had existed since at least 1513, when Vasco Núñez de Balboa, a Spanish conquistador, first climbed the mountains of Panama and saw the Pacific Ocean on the other side.

When the French started building the canal in 1881, they underestimated the obstacles posed by the rain forest, the mountains, and disease. After seventeen years they gave up, and the U.S. took over the project. Some people argued that Nicaragua would be a better site. But once the U.S. Congress decided on the shorter route through Panama, no effort was spared.

Slides were the biggest challenge of the construction. Steam shovels worked feverishly to slice off the top of the Cut, but that wasn't enough. In 1912, the YMCA, ICC headquarters, and other buildings in Culebra had to be dismantled and moved to keep them from sliding into the Cut. In January of the next year, Cucaracha deposited almost half a million cubic yards of fill into the Cut, and three days later another million cubic feet gave way nearby.

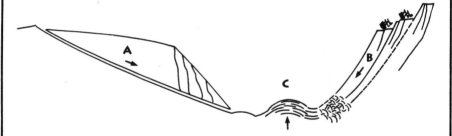

SLIDES IN CULEBRA CUT

Slide A, like the one at Cucaracha, is caused by slow-creeping wet clay. Slide B, like the one that trapped William and Victoria, occurs when the weight of the soil causes the cliff to break away. (Terracing at the top of the cliff takes off some of the weight.) The high speed of the moving soil forces the floor of the Cut upward at C.

That autumn Colonel Goethals ordered the Cut flooded and the rest of the spoil removed by dredges. But the slides continued, and by 1914, the U.S. had removed over 25 million cubic yards of spoil from slides alone—over one-fourth of the total U.S. excavation. In all, the price tag for Culebra Cut was over ten million dollars a mile.

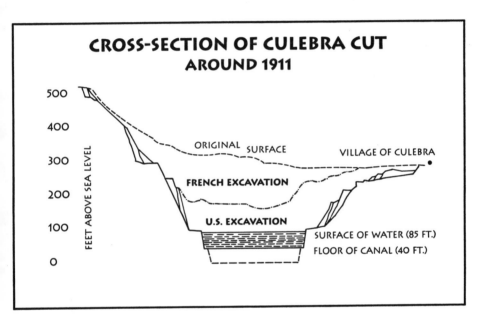

So few people lived on the isthmus that assembling the labor to build the canal was another major challenge. At the height of construction, about fifty thousand people were employed by the ICC. More than twenty-five thousand of them were from Barbados, Jamaica, and other islands of the West Indies. These people were paid only about $25 a month, which was far more than jobs at home paid but far less than other canal workers were paid. The five thousand white Americans on the ICC payroll earned an average of $150 a month. Steam-shovel operators earned about twice that amount.

Many workers died from yellow fever and malaria, especially during the early years of construction. The U.S. made controlling these diseases a priority and was so effective at eliminating them (and the mosquitoes that spread them) that eventually pneumonia and tuberculosis replaced yellow fever and malaria as the most common illnesses in the Canal Zone. Despite these efforts, 5,500 workers died of disease between 1904 and 1914, eighty percent of whom were from the West Indies.

The Panama Canal opened to shipping in August 1914, six months ahead of schedule. However, the fanfare was not as great as expected, because the world's attention was focused on Europe, where the Great War, later called World War I, had just erupted.

Culebra Cut was renamed Gaillard Cut in honor of its chief engineer, David D. Gaillard, who had died of a brain tumor in December 1913. Even after the canal was open to traffic, Gaillard Cut was closed several times to clear slides, once as recently as 1974.

About twelve thousand ships a year take the eight-hour trip through the canal. Some vessels, particularly petroleum supertankers, are too large for the locks and must still travel around the tip of South America.

At noon on December 31, 1999, the U.S. lease on the canal expires, and ownership will pass to the Republic of Panama. The building of the canal remains the largest construction feat in history, an example of what dreams, careful plans, and hard work can accomplish.

HOW THE CANAL WORKS

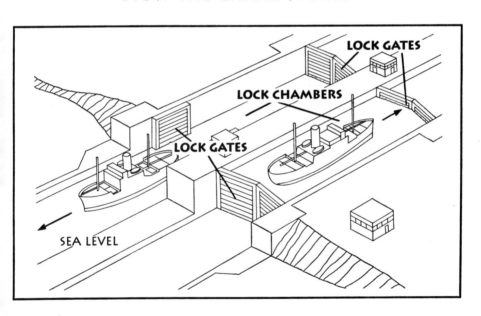

When a ship enters the canal from either ocean, a gate closes behind it and the lock chamber fills with water, lifting the boat as it fills. When the water level reaches that of the next chamber, a gate opens to allow the ship to progress. The second and third locks work the same way, lifting the ship to 85 feet above sea level—high enough for the vessel to pass through Culebra Cut without scraping the bottom 45 feet below.

When the ship enters the locks at the other end of the canal, the water in each chamber drains out and returns the ship to sea level so it can sail out into the other ocean.

For information and advice that shaped this book, the author is especially grateful to rain forest biologist Joanne Sharpe; historians Avi Chomsky, Margaret Creighton, and Michael E. Jones of Bates College; Jamaicans Barbara Carnegie and David Scott; editor Jill Anderson; Jo Ellen Head, Susan Allison, Carolyn Crocker, Betsy Hanscom, and Deb Shumaker.